OIL & GASOLINE

OIL & GASOLINE

A story of two survivors

Billi Gordon & Taylor-Anne Wentworth

Boston • Alyson Publications, Inc.

Other books by Billi Gordon:

You've Had Worse Things in Your Mouth Cookbook
Eat This Book: The Last Diet Book
Your Moon Is in Aquarius But Your Head Is in Uranus

Typeset and printed in the United States of America.

This is a paperback original from Alyson Publications, Inc.,
40 Plympton St., Boston, Mass. 02118.
Distributed in England by GMP Publishers,
P.O. Box 247, London N17 9QR England.

This book is printed on acid-free, recycled paper.

First edition, first printing: November 1991

5 4 3 2 1

ISBN 1-55583-191-5

Taylor-Anne Wentworth
wishes to extend special thanks to her two muses,
Scott Tyson and Peter Isgro
of Isgro & Co.

Billi Gordon
wishes to extend her special thanks to
James Toy
of the University of Michigan
for helping her to find the courage to live.

Both authors wish to extend their deep thanks to
Sasha Alyson
of Alyson Publications
for having the courage to publish this book.

This story is largely autobiographical. However, certain characters and events were created for dramatic and literary purposes.

This is for
every devastated child who has fallen to incest,
and for every adult who has fallen to a devastated child.

October 25

Dear Diary,

I am in the grips of grief. I just got back from two months at MacQuiddy Lake helping to take care of Kip's dying father. I liked my father-in-law, Hunter, and the two months went fast. Not so much because of my love for Hunter, but because of my sister-in-law, Carolyn. Isn't death supposed to be tragic and trying on one's nerves? Why then did I and Carolyn-of-four-husbands have such a great time?

Aren't you supposed to hate your sister-in-law? Kip and I have only three months of marriage under our belts, so how would I know? Aren't writers supposed to hate other writers? Well, whatever the rules are, Carolyn and I broke them and had a great time doing so.

Well, all except that dreadful, goddamned, knobby-kneed, Popsicle-breathed, Bazooka-bubble-blowing, motley Molly that lives next door to Carolyn.

I hate children. They're too much like cameras ... painfully truthful. They're worse than cameras actually, 'cause the painful truth of cameras can be avoided by simply not allowing oneself to be photographed. But children are another story all together. I go to the supermarket and here comes some little Popsicle-stained brat with Cheerios on his breath, saying, "Mommy, how come that lady doesn't have a neck?" Or they'll come right up to you and say something like "Ma'am, how come the backs of your thighs are so lumpy?" And just like that, with one vile, foul, disgusting scrape with truth, innocence, and a cartoon t-shirt, I am left limp with indecision for life. Which is worse? Doing jail time for drop-kicking a child from the cereal aisle into the frozen peas, having cottage cheese thighs, or being called "ma'am"?

Anyhow, I have a doctor's appointment today. You see, I've been imagining all of these smells. Everywhere I go, I'm always smelling oil and gasoline, and minerals and things. And if I'm not smelling oil and gasoline, I'm tasting blood or some strange salty substance. Oops, look at the time! I'm running late ... I'll write more later.

Hi, I'm back from the doctor. Dr. Hickman thinks that I might have a brain tumor. I can't believe this. I'm thirty-two years old. I just published my third book, co-starred in my first major film, married a great guy, met the best friend of my life, and now ... I'm going to die. All my life I've contemplated suicide and just when I have something to live for ... this! I don't want to die now. I'm not ready yet.

Ruby Rae

October 28

Dearest sister-in-law and best friend,

Thank you for your constant and patient help in caring for my father as he succumbed to the final stages of cancer. Without you, caring for Hunter in our home would have proved overwhelming, since like you, Rick and I have more than full-time careers. (Although people up here do question mine, since I write all day and haven't yet reached the point of being published. It's only now that you're at home in Los Angeles, which is a good four hundred miles from here on MacQuiddy Lake, that I dare admit I'm envious that you've published three books, and in two years I've yet to finish my first.)

That for eight weeks you were able to empty bedpans and wash soiled sheets in a manner that enabled you and Hunter to maintain your dignity tells me you're a very special person. I'm particularly grateful to you for taking the "night shift" during Hunter's last week, and for being willing to give him his morphine. And a huge double thanks for getting the priest when Hunter was ready for him. Of all of us, you were the most attuned to Hunter's need to resolve his differences with the Catholic Church. Had he not received the final Sacrament of Absolution, he never would have come to grips with his fear of death and dying.

In many ways, you were much more helpful than my brother, Kip. Of course, he's a man. And men are never there for you in the ways you need them. Trust me, after eighteen years of life with a father like Hunter (if you can call what we had back then "life") I know all about this. But then, when is time on Earth ever ideal?

Nevertheless, I often felt angry when I nursed Hunter. Your presence checked my rage and prevented me from walking from his grave with regrets. It's much better that I overinvested in caring for him, than have his death leave me with the remorse of things unsaid or undone.

This isn't to say that caring for Hunter didn't have benefits. Watching him die eased my own fears about death and dying. And, as an orthopedic surgeon, Rick had his first real experience with the practical problems of home care. He is now more sensitive to the social and physical needs of his homebound patients and their caregivers. But for me, the best thing that came from this experience was getting to know you. (It's so very refreshing to at last meet someone who understands that friendship is more than a card at Christmas and a promise to do lunch.) After all the late-night talks we shared while we sat outside Hunter's bedroom, we're destined to be more than in-laws: we're destined to be lifelong friends.

So how about celebrating an old-fashioned Thanksgiving with your new northern California family? (It comes so early this year! The twenty-second!) We'll bake pies, and make rolls from scratch, and watch the Macy's Parade in our flannel nightgowns and those matching elephant slippers we bought to raise our spirits the day after Hunter died. While the men watch football, we'll sit in the kitchen, and share deep secrets and risqué jokes in the way that only best friends and soul sisters can. Write soon! I miss you!

Love and hugs,
Your sister, Carolyn

P.S. I spent the morning getting out the monthly statements to Rick's patients rather than writing. Sometimes, I wonder if Rick has any idea how much money and time I save him by working at his office twelve hours a week. And the Mrs. Doctors wonder what I do with my time!

November 5

Dear Diary,

Drapes! Floor-length black drapes! I just got back from the doctor. He wants to run some more tests, but he's 90 percent positive that I have a brain tumor. Wouldn't you just know it? I don't want anyone to know I'm dying. Especially Kip and Carolyn. They just went through so much pain with the loss of their father. I don't want to put them through that pain, again. Not now. Not so soon. I have to distance myself from Carolyn, so that when the inevitable happens it won't be so painful for her. It'll be easier for me, too. As for Kip, when the time is right I'll let him know. There's really no way to gradually distance yourself from your husband.

Anyway, Carolyn is not going to make it easy for me to bow out of this friendship gracefully. Those matching elephant slippers were the kiss of death. Curse you, Macy's, and the bitch in the bun who sold us those slippers! Well, regardless of how much Carolyn likes me, and I like her, I'm doing this for her own good ... Come up and share deep secrets; no, I don't think so.

I have it. Carolyn doesn't really know me. She just thinks I'm this chic authoress and actress her brother married. I try to be that. I try with all of my might to be that. Nobody knows where I really come from, and who I really am, though. I never wanted anybody to find out. Especially Carolyn. When she finds out where I came from, she will run for the country club. I'm going to write her a letter that will blow the buttons off of her Chanel suit ... and then she'll leave me alone. But first a little toddy.

Ruby Rae

P.S. I'm glad watching Hunter die eased Carolyn's fear of death and dying. Personally, it made mine worse. The thought of lying in bed, riddled with pain, gasping for breath, too weak to talk, much less scream, and waiting on some bitch like me to bring me my morphine, when I just know she's in the cupboards appraising my silver, is scary, truly scary.

November 5

Dear Carolyn,

I'm glad I was able to help Hunter mend his break with the Catholic Church because of Vatican II. I'm happy he could die in peace. I feel deeply for all of those Catholics that the Church left marooned and orphaned with the travesty of Vatican II. And I do feel like Hunter, when he would bark, "I didn't leave the Church ... the Church left me." Nonetheless, to a good Catholic, the Last Sacraments are important ... and if we were alike in no other way, Hunter and I were good Catholics.

Anyway, I'm sitting here looking through Kip's old photos from childhood. They're pretty different from mine. The house I grew up in was a tar paper shack on a dirt street, across from the city dump, on the wrong side of a little blue-collar, southern Michigan town called Tucker. It was as pitiful-looking as the poster baby for some famine relief campaign. It wasn't at all like your big white mansion, Villa Adagio, on Sant' Andrea Place overlooking the Bel-Air Country Club golf course.

My daddy's name was Willie, and he worked in a steel mill. He had those big, rough hands with the kind of dirt under their fingernails that no amount of Boraxo could ever get out. I can still smell the oil, coal dust, graphite, and gasoline on his work jeans. I still can see my mamma — her name was Catfyshe — standing at the washing machine, wearing red patent leather spikes and a black slip with a Lucky Strike in one hand and a box of Tide in the other, singing, "I got an itch ... but it ain't nowhere you can scratch..." while trying to get out the ground-in iron ore and manganese from Willie's dungarees.

Granted, I am a successful authoress and actress now, but the reality is, I'm still from across the tracks and it's a long way from South Slag Alley to Sant' Andrea Place, as Kip's fond strolls through his childhood memories constantly remind me.

I have childhood memories, too. I remember when Catfyshe found Willie's mistress's panties in the car, and greeted him at the door with a shotgun in one hand and those panties in the other. She shot him through the shoulder. Then she threw the panties on his chest and said, "Wipe up the blood with these, motherfucker! They might be dry enough by now!"

I remember shortly thereafter visiting Catfyshe at the jail. Well, trying to visit Catfyshe at the jail. She was actually out the day we came, having an ice cream with a sympathetic young cop who she "knew," so to speak.

Catfyshe drank a lot of vodka, and always straight, and always until there was no more and no money to be found. You see, the men just called my mamma "Brick," shortened from "brick shit house," as in "she's built like a brick shit house." The women just called Mamma "shit house." I'll admit she was a big-tittied, drunken, man-stealing, back-alley, wayward, miniskirt-wearin', raw-wienie-eating woman (Catfyshe loved to eat cold hot dogs right out of the package, walking or driving down the street) ... that was real strange to most folks ... to me that was just Mamma.

Catfyshe preferred to think of herself as just a "pretty, big-legged thang" that men just couldn't resist. That's what she'd say, then she'd cross her legs and say, "I'm in the mood for an Italian" ... Or she'd get up, throw open the curtains, and say, "What a beautiful day! Makes me feel like doing a lawyer ... wonder what Jeff's up to?" ... Or she'd yawn, and stretch out on the couch on her stomach while reading the phone book, and say, "Ummm, George and Sarah Johnson ... they seem like a happy couple ... we'll just see about that." Then she'd roll over onto her back, light a cigarette, and run her long nails through her long hair, kinda purr, kinda growl, kinda like a little ol' kitten, kinda like a big ol' cat, and say, "'Cause I feel like breaking up somebody's home."

Take care,
Ruby Rae

November 10

Dear, dear Ruby Rae,

First off, in this day and age, we delete all the "esses." The politically correct terms for your job titles are author and actor. Second, don't be impressed by the Villa Adagio. Our parents, Hunter and Portia, only rented the mansion for twenty-eight years. And third, I feel closer to you than ever. I'm so very touched (not to mention relieved) that our childhoods were stitched together with the same colored threads: black, and blue, and green. (Strange, isn't it, that up until now neither of us realized our backgrounds are similar? People who call their parents by their first names usually either come from very liberal, or very dysfunctional, homes. And while our parents may have been a lot of things, liberal was not among them.)

Granted, there's good to be found in just about anything. But it floors me that Kip hasn't also spoken of the darker moments in that leaky-roofed house on Sant' Andrea Place. I know men process events and experiences in ways that are peculiar and different from women, but I never dreamed their processing could be so slanted. Then again, this may have nothing to do with sex-linked traits. This may just prove how well I protected him from what went down in the Villa Adagio.

To begin with, our mother, Portia, was a junkie. Well, not a junkie-junkie. Portia had too much class for that, she was a "chemical dependent." Personally, I think the only difference between a junkie and a chemical dependent is the street on which they live.

Portia got hooked at eighteen when she wanted to shed a few pounds. She had heard weight loss was easy with the right kind of pills, and returned from a visit to her family doc with a no-refill prescription for Methedrine and instructions to exercise. She threw out the mandate for sweat when she discovered the pills' great kick.

When she was out of pills, there was no going back to the physician who advised her to exercise. So she turned to another practitioner, who was known to enjoy afternoon cocktails. Again, she got another unsatisfactory prescription: a no-refill order for sixty hits of speed. Portia decided this just wouldn't do and added a second zero to the authorized number of pills.

Naturally, Portia was questioned by the pharmacist about the prescription. Of course, he phoned the prescribing physician. But the call was placed in late afternoon, and by then the doctor had had a few cocktails. With the aid of a few martinis, he authorized the disbursement of six hundred hits of speed and launched Portia down a path of no return.

Needless to say, the pills didn't do a thing for Portia's personality, which we all suspect developed from a core inclined toward bitchy. At my birth, she was eight years into her habit. Six years later she gave birth to the twins, Grace and Kip, after she sensed the need to anchor Hunter to their house with a few more children. (At the time, Hunter's relationship with his then-current mistress had grown a tad too serious.)

The new offspring met Portia when her body was tired and worn from being at the height of its habit. Her mood swings were faster, her rages were more fierce, and her knack for twisting reality was more finely tuned during Kip and Grace's preschool years than during mine.

When I was thirteen, the police made two visits to our house. I had the luck to answer the door both times (as well as the good sense to suspect that what they had to offer could be worse than anything Portia could dish out). I shook off the devout Catholic-schooled child in me to invent a line that explained the shouting and violence with the statement that Grace, my retarded sister, lived with us. I said her face was black-and-blue from slamming it through her bedroom's shutters.

Had the police asked Grace to open her mouth, they would have also seen her gums, which were red and swollen from the splinters embedded in them. At the time, she had the habit of chewing on the Louis XV headboard of her bed. Naturally, her behavior incensed Portia. Like the Villa Adagio, every plate, every fork, every mug, every glass, every antique, every clock and painting, and any and all sticks of furniture that graced its interior were rented. And Hunter lacked the funds to pay for the restoration of the antique bed that Grace damaged.

Hunter coped with the combined disasters of Portia's pills and Grace's challenge by setting up a network of reliable mistresses. As one would expect, none of those vamps were any gems. And, as one would expect, Hunter would, every now and then, attempt to leave Portia for one of them.

Once Grace's challenge presented itself, Portia no longer viewed another pregnancy as the best means for keeping her husband. So she resorted to slashing Hunter's wrist, or pouring hot coffee in his crotch while she brought up the always delicate issue of money when Hunter spoke of leaving her. Without Portia's family jewels and silver to pawn, there was no guarantee that the car payments, rent, and full-time housekeeper could be paid, or that Hunter could maintain his business office. Thus, our parents remained married not for the children, but for the family jewels and silver.

To her Bel-Air and Beverly Hills set, Portia was charming, and beautiful, and rich, and well dressed, and fun, and just too wonderfully perfect! But then, Portia never invited anyone from her set to our house. (Strange, isn't it, that the more distanced a person is, the more revered they become?) At her funeral, her friends repeatedly remarked to me that they'd never heard her say a cross word. And each time, I thought, How sad. Portia wasn't sufficiently secure in herself to disagree with a woman she'd known for thirty years, but she never missed an opportunity to batter her kids.

Oh, and speaking of kids, our next-door neighbor, Meg, just hired yet another *au pair* for Molly, her five-year-old daughter. This new "mother's helper" is named Olga, and she comes from one of those Slavic countries. Molly just came by here in tears, because she was starving to death. Olga has such a poor grasp of English that she couldn't understand Molly when she begged for an after-school snack.

Anyway, I dried Molly's eyes, sat her down at the kitchen table, and brought out a bag of chocolate-covered Oreos. We spent a happy half-hour dunking the cookies in milk and talking things over. When I promised to bake her chocolate chip cookies tomorrow, her eyes absolutely sparkled! Why would anyone hire an *au pair* who can barely speak English? What if something happens to Molly, and 911 needs to be called? You would think that her mother, Meg-the-attorney, would be more on the ball!

Love you,
Carolyn

P.S. Oh! I almost forgot. Molly just adores that lipstick you gave her. She told me to tell you she only uses it on her very "bestest" dolls because the "grown-up" color better suits them than her.

November 15

Dear Diary,

The sky is crying. And I'm sitting here, with my best friend, Jack ... Daniels, that is, watching the teardrops roll on down the street into a gutter that empties into the creek, that flows into a river, that slides into the sea. A salty sea of blues that's washing over me.

I got my diagnosis today. My doctor says I have a brain tumor and that I am going to die. He wants me to go see this specialist, though, because the brain tumor is not showing up on any of the scans or X-rays, but the symptoms are proof positive as far as we are concerned ... The smelling of false smells, the tasting of false tastes. I'm going down. Why do they tell people that they're going to die? Why don't they either shoot them in the head or just leave them alone?

Plus, my plan with Carolyn totally backfired. Not only did I not blow the buttons off of her Chanel suit ... I ended up with my own panties in a bundle. Boy, some of the things Carolyn said brought tears to my eyes. I feel closer to her than ever ... damn it!

And Kip just accepted an invitation to go to her house for Thanksgiving ... without discussing it with me, of course. This is not getting any easier. I don't want to have a tumor attack while I'm up there, and be left at the mercy of Rick. God knows, Carolyn could have leprosy and he'd never know it. He's never there, and I think he was at the bottom of his class in medical school. I don't need her overworked, underfed husband digging around in my head!

And that bug-eyed, licorice-lipped Molly is so nosy, and there are things besides this tumor that I don't want Carolyn to find out about. The last time I was at Carolyn's, that Molly used my last nerve for a trampoline. Not to mention the little heifer got in my purse and stole my favorite lipstick — Make Mine Chocolate by Dark and Luscious — and had the nerve to tell Carolyn I gave it to her.

Molly hates me. She's jealous of me and Carolyn. She considers herself "Carolyn's bestest friend." And I don't like her mother either...

Nosdrovia,
Ruby Rae

November 16

Dear Carolyn,

First of all, I have had to drop more than just the "esses" over the years to ensure my success and freedom. And nothing personal, but I am not the least bit interested in what current gestures white suburban feminists are putting themselves through to feel liberated. As an artist of color, I am too busy fighting an oppression that I feel comes at least as much from white women as from white men.

Secondly, don't tell me that I finally get to come uptown and it's on trash night. How dare you tell Catfyshe Stone's baby child something like this? Do you know how long I've been trying to escape the wrong side of the tracks and all of its subsequent depravity?

Are you on drugs, or is there a toxic waste dump on MacQuiddy Lake? This can't be the truth! You're from "What if the American dream comes true" hill. Your reality is worse than the grim fact that one size does not fit all, and Molly's mother is never going to move. (Just kidding — I know how you love "Molly-the-Magnificent.")

Anyway, the kind of things you're talking about is the kind of stuff that Catfyshe and Willie were doing across the tracks back in Tucker. I'll never forget the time Big Katie Mae, the neighbor lady, came over to our house to see Catfyshe. She was a big, tall, pigeon-toed woman. Katie Mae was crying. She told Catfyshe she was frightened because Little Joe Henry, her old man, was having an affair. Catfyshe was sitting at her dressing table, naked, powdering her body with a long-handled, oversized powder puff. She stopped powdering herself for a moment and asked, "Do you know who with?" Katie Mae told Mamma she didn't know who with, but she just knew. Mamma started powdering her shoulders again and asked, "Do you give him good booty, girl?" Katie Mae looked confused, and finally said, "Well, of course I do." Mamma put down her big powder puff and said, "Well, don't worry then, if the booty's good, he'll be back." Then she gave her a bottle of her favorite perfume, Tabu, and said, "Spray yourself, down there, with this tonight when he comes home and he'll be all over you." So Katie Mae left. When Mamma was sure she was gone, she said, "Okay, you can come out now," and Little Joe Henry stepped out of Mamma's closet. He said, "I can't believe you told my wife if the booty's good, I'll be back." Mamma looked at him, paused for a second, then said, "Well, you're back, aren't you?"

There were no police then, acting like some child protective agency. I wish there had been. If only someone had come to our door, I would've jumped in their arms. Like the time when Catfyshe stabbed me in the wrist with that butcher knife, or beat me in the face with the naked mop handle, or threw me out into the snow at midnight, stark naked. If only, but no. Only the police came. And they just talked to Brick, gave me a Tootsie Roll Pop, and "forgot" to make out a report.

But it's like that in little towns. In little towns, you pay your bills, accept things, and don't talk about them. "Brick's nervous," they used to say in Tucker. A more accurate clinical description of my mother was: an alcoholic, manic-depressive obsessive-compulsive with a critically low self-esteem.

But I just can't believe what I'm hearing about your family. I always thought that everything was okay in your family. Everybody always spoke of your family as "the perfect family." It's comforting in a morose sort of way to know that Portia didn't wake up with every hair in place, wearing a simple strand of pearls, like June Cleaver. Then again, it's sad, 'cause I guess I wonder, where was that street that the Cleavers, the Nelsons, and the Andersons lived on? I guess in light of all of this, we may not be so different after all. I'm so glad you convinced Kip to come up for Thanksgiving.

All my heart...
Ruby Rae

November 26

Dear Diary,

I survived Thanksgiving at Carolyn's, no thanks to Molly-the-sticky-pawed-nosy-motley. I hate children. The truth darts from their lips like daggers. And if you're not careful they can destroy a girl's world just like that. "You look fatter" and "Why are your eyes so red?" were the first words out of her lollipop-licking lips.

Anyway. Back to the real world: my fading life. I went to the specialist. Dr. Sonae Fujita. She's Japanese. I don't like having a woman doctor, and I don't like having one whose parents bombed Pearl Harbor. I mean, I'm as liberal as they come. If this was a routine checkup, fine. But a brain tumor is serious business. I need a serious doctor. I need an old white man. I don't believe I just wrote that. I don't believe I just thought that. Nothing like extreme fear to bring out the truth. And speaking of truth: there must be some truth to the saying "It's not what white men think about us that's the problem ... it's what they've taught us to think about ourselves that's the problem."

Dr. Fujita says that Dr. Hickman's tests were inconclusive. She was testing me and taking blood all afternoon. What for? For all I know she could be collecting props for the next King Kong movie. Anyhow, I ran into Dr. Hickman at the liquor store. I told him what Dr. Fujita said, about his findings being "inconclusive," and he said, "If it looks like vodka, smells like vodka, and tastes like vodka, I say it is vodka, and you, my dear, have a brain tumor. Now pass me that gallon of vodka."

I don't know who's right. But we all agree that something is wrong with me and it's serious. I'm scared, very scared. I saw what a tumor did to Hunter.

Anyway, Thanksgiving dinner was adequate. Carolyn's gravy was okay, but that stuffing ... who's ever heard of grapes in stuffing? And I gotta tell ya, Carolyn's taste in decorating ... it looks like the Museum for Old Caucasians up there. Still I had fun. Lots of fun. Too much fun.

Thank God, I won't have to deal with Carolyn, other than by letter, for many months. Such a mixed blessing. I don't need the frustration, and she doesn't need to get any closer to me, in light of this tumor or whatever it is. And since I am dying, there are things about my life that I'd just rather she and my husband never know. Things ... I'd like to forget.

Ruby Rae

November 26

Dear Carolyn,

I just wanted to drop you this little note and say thank you for a lovely Thanksgiving. Everything was truly wonderful, and I can't remember when I've had a better meal. Such interesting stuffing. I've never had better turkey gravy in my life. It was really nice being at your house under pleasant circumstances, and I love what you've done with the place. You've captured the essence of traditional. And that Molly, she's sooooo cute. Oh, look at the time! I have to rush off to the gym to do my workout. I'll see ya later.

Love ya,
Ruby Rae

November 27

Dear Diary,

I just got back from the gym. I'm wrecked. Do you hear me? Wrecked! I gained 8 pounds over Thanksgiving! How could I have gained 8 pounds on a white woman's cooking? How? How could anybody gain that much weight in just four days? It must be the tumor. That's what Dr. Hickman says.

I just want to go inside of myself and cut this tumor out. I feel the way Catfyshe must have felt the time she tried to cut off Willie's penis ... because a *Readers' Digest* article said, when a married couple is having problems, the wife should find the source of the problem, and get rid of it.

Ruby Rae

November 29

Ruby Rae,

I guess the term "interesting" explains why you shared your modest helping of Thanksgiving stuffing with the potted palm by your chair at the dining room table. And don't you dare try to weasel your way onto on my good side by pleading ill health and then asking for my old family recipe! I only made that stuffing because I assumed you are as fond of the grape in its natural state as you are of it in its fermented form. Besides, how was I to know that someone who lives on fried food, pickled pigs' lips, and pork rinds (oh, pardon me, "skins") would be soooo particular about what she ingests?

And speaking of eating, I have another bone to pick. When Molly so innocently observed that you'd gotten "more fluffy" since your last visit, you behaved exactly like Portia behaved whenever she topped the scale at a hundred and one pounds: you ran to the nearest john and poked your finger down your throat till you started blowing chunks. (Unfortunately, for those of us who were on the other side of the bathroom's closed door, the tub's gushing tap didn't mask the sound.) Don't you know that unless you improve your self-image, you could wake up tomorrow wearing a size four like Portia, and still feel too insecure to turn down any dates with Jim Beam? This rather conveniently brings me to topic number three.

Molly did a treasure hunt in our yard this afternoon (her class is collecting recyclable items for a fund-raiser), and lo and behold! Guess what treasures she found? That's right, the dozen empty quart bottles of Jack Daniels that were hidden in the shrubs just outside our guest room's window. (She also found a fifth of Boone's Farm Apple Wine, which I munificently assumed was left by the gardener.) Of course, she wanted to bag the lot, and trot them off to school. But we could hardly have that with this being a small town! Gracious! I couldn't even bring myself to dump them in the trash! La Scandal! La Embarrassment!

Fortunately, I had the presence of mind to give Molly ten dollars toward her fund-raiser. Then, I dragged the collection down into the wine cellar. You can take the bounty back to L.A. after your next visit. Oh, and by the way, do you know that drinkers who hide their bottles, and their need for an hourly fix, also hide other things? (Including the calories they intake when they party with those Daniels brothers, Black and Green!)

A very disappointed (but still loving),
Carolyn

P.S. On a lighter note, I really appreciate the comments you made about the short story I finished. When I finish the rewrite, you can give it to your agent, if you will be so kind. Also, I took your advice, and mailed off my application to join that writers' group at the local university. As you so wisely said, being around other artists will help me feel more connected to the people up here.

December 1

Dear Ruby Rae,

I'm sorry my last letter was a tad harsh. I meant everything I wrote, but I regret my tone, and the fact I left out the most important part: I loved having you here.

As for me, my "dance card" is full for the next ten days, so it might be best if you didn't write. I won't have time to read your letters. I'd hate for you to waste your time writing me, when you could be working on your book.

Carolyn

December 4

Dear Diary,

I just got back from the specialist. Some specialist. She says, and I quote, "You have all of the symptoms of a brain tumor, but you don't have a brain tumor ... I don't know why this is." She's referred me to some more doctors for new tests. She also suggested that I see a shrink! Please! I'm a successful author for God's sake. I'm not crazy, I'm just near death and in no mood. Plus, I just got another letter from Carolyn. After that last self-righteous letter of hers ... just because she and that long-nosed Molly found an empty bottle or two of my tumor medicine in her bushes ... I decided to not even open this one. I just sent it back to her, "addressee in no mood." I am over her and that Molly-the-mangy. Carolyn would've never found those bottles in the bushes if not for Molly. If Molly wants to be a bloodhound so bad, then why don't they put some spots on her, give her a tail, and send her to work at Scotland Yard? Skoal, darling!

Ruby Rae

December 5

Dear Diary,

Strangest thing, I just got a message on my answering machine from Rick ... Carolyn's Rick ... saying when Carolyn arrives have her give him a call. He must be working too hard ... as usual. Carolyn couldn't be coming here. Carolyn and I haven't communicated in a long time and Carolyn would never show up unannounced. Especially in light of the fact that we're fighting.

Cheers,
Ruby Rae

Dear Diary,

Twice in one day, how about that? This letter, like my Jack Daniels, is for medicinal purposes, however. I just got a message on my answering machine from Carolyn! Rick wasn't overworked after all. She left a number. She's in L.A.! I wonder why? This is strange. Of course, I did send her last letter back ... Anyway, she left a number with an extension and said call her as soon as possible. She also said that she didn't want Rick to know where she is. She said she was a fool not to have worked this out with me before she left. I don't know what's going on, Rick already knows she's here.

Here's looking at you,
Ruby Rae

Dear Diary,

Three times in one day. No, I didn't call *Guinness* ... yet. I just got off of the phone with Carolyn. She's in the hospital! UCLA. That's where I have to go to have my tests! If it wasn't for bad luck, I wouldn't have any luck at all!

Now why isn't she in St. John's, where her family always goes? She says she's not in the Neuropsychiatric Institute (where my next series of tests are) ... and she didn't have a car accident ... hmmmm. All she said was that her condition was not the kind of thing you went to St. John's for. What does she mean by that? I'll write more later.

Well, it's later and I'm writing more. You won't believe this. Carolyn's down here having an abortion. And not only is she having an abortion, but she has talked her gynecologist into sterilizing her vaginally at the same time. She doesn't want any scars.

Being sterilized and having an abortion all at the same time is very dangerous, because there's a high rate of infection. I don't know what's wrong with Carolyn. I don't know how she talked her gynecologist into it. He must be a man. And God knows, if anybody would be comfortable in the stirrups with a man, it would be Carolyn.

How can I joke about this? This is terrible. Plus, it doesn't make any sense. Carolyn loves children. Anybody who could love Molly has to love children. 'Cause God knows Molly is the strongest argument for birth control that I've run into in a while. This calls for some tumor medicine.

Ruby Rae

December 6

Dear Carolyn,

I'm sending you these flowers not because I approve of what you're doing. They are not an apology either for walking out of the hospital on you. Partially they are to congratulate you on making an application to the writers' group. Partially ... just because.

Anyway ... You know as a devout Catholic and a former member of a religious order, there is no way I can aid in your abortion in any way. By covering up for your deed, I'm a part of it, and I can't justify that morally. No, I will not lie to Rick for you. Not for this.

I'm not going to lecture you about family, family values, mortal sins, or the value of the family unit — just because I believe in preserving it at all costs. You went to Catholic school; you were taught by the nuns; you know better; this is between you and God ... just as my relationship with God would never allow me personally to have any part in any abortion. Now I understand why you couldn't go to St. John's. I will do this, however: I will make a novena for you and the soul of your murdered child.

Ruby Rae

December 6

Dear Diary,

The hospital is releasing Carolyn. She just called to see if she can stay with me until she gets well enough to drive home. I had to resort to pretending to be a righteous Catholic, which I sorta am, to try to get out of helping her. It's not that I'm anti-choice when it comes to abortion and sterilization, but there are two issues here.

Number one, I know Carolyn is lonely and a child could be just the thing that her life is lacking. So this decision seems irrational.

Number two, honey, I'm too close to going to see My Maker to gamble with the teachings of the Mother Church now. And that's just the truth. I mean, please, you can't ask a Catholic kid to get involved in an abortion on her death-bed. Not now ... maybe last year ... but not now. No, not until this tumor thing is completely worked out.

Then again, I suppose there would be nothing too wrong with letting Carolyn come stay with me, until she heals. I mean, I do want to help her, I just hate to spend an eternity in hell for it. Maybe I'll make myself a toddy and research this in the *Baltimore Catechism.*

Ruby Rae

December 7

Dear Carolyn,

Maybe the lateness of the hour makes me feel more genuine than I really am. Maybe the brightness of the moon makes me see things that always remained in darkness, that I seldom had the need to understand. Nonetheless, for some reason, I feel compelled to help you. Now that you are fighting this awful infection, which is the risk everybody told you about ... but I won't go into that.

Yes, you can come tomorrow and stay with me until you heal. However, I am not speaking to you. I'm taking care of you because you're Kip's sister and because according to the *Baltimore Catechism* it's my duty as a good Catholic to perform the Corporal Works of Mercy, which include caring for the sick ... no matter how heathen they might be.

Although I have nothing to say to you, I'm sure you'll have plenty to say to me. Therefore, we can communicate by note. Furthermore, I am much too busy a career woman to be cleaning house all day. And I know what you're going to try. You're going to break out in hives and your fever is going to go up the first minute a little dust hits the lamp shade. Well, save your mercury. I will not be bullied by your infirmity.

Another thing. When I was a guest at your house, I let you bully me into folding towels and sheets your way. However, now that you're in my house, the towels and sheets will be folded the correct way. The way Mother Mary Timothy and Sister Barbara Marie taught me in the convent.

Thank you very much,
Ruby Rae

December 12

Dear Ruby Rae,

I will leave for home tomorrow morning. Although the rapid improvement of my health can probably be attributed to the fact that I haven't had to talk to you while I've been here, I suspect your vow of silence has had a drawback or two for you. Just because you won't talk to me, it doesn't mean I didn't hear you walk up to my closed bedroom door and eavesdrop on all of my phone conversations with Rick. You may be a lot of things, but between your copious hips and your wide-bodied feet that you stack on those six-inch high heels, you are not (I repeat, not) Twinkle Toes.

I know it kills you not to know what Rick said to me during those long, long, long pauses you heard when you listened to me listen to him on the phone last night. So, I will tell you this much: if you think I'm leaving a day early because of your cooking, if that's the word for what you do to food with a stove, think again. I'd love to be a bit more specific about the real reason I'm leaving, but it's soooo hard to be more specific when we aren't speaking. (And if curiosity is about to kill you like some cat, do remember, satisfaction brings cats back. Just say, "meow," and I'll know you're ready to be revived.)

I deeply appreciate your promise not to tell anyone about my visit to UCLA. You don't have to be Sherlock Holmes to figure out I told Rick I got my period, when I didn't. But what Mr. Holmes and others like him may not know is that this was the hardest thing I have ever done in my life. I never thought I would get pregnant, so I never prepared myself for the consequences of lying to my husband about something as important as this. I think I've told a million lies in the past few weeks. Lying makes me want to wash my hands until they become so rough and red my skin peels off.

I also appreciate your willingness to lead Kip to believe I came to L.A. for some plastic surgery. (Oh, and a triple thanks for the use of your old bra, and that big box of tissues. The minute I get home, I'm going to phone down here and tell Kip my new boobies deflated. I'll just say they collapsed when my car hit one of those huge potholes on the interstate. Kip will feel so sorry for me that he'll be more than willing to promise not to mention my failed surgery to Rick. I know I can depend on you to be a dear, and back up my story.)

Anyway, since your morals would only allow you to interact with me to the point of placing me at risk of getting food poisoning, I have no other choice but to write my thanks for letting me stay here, and for nursing me back to health. I also want to explain why I decided to have an abortion and be sterilized. Please understand, I don't feel I owe you an explanation. I want to tell you, because you are my closest sister and dearest friend. The truth will build a bridge of understanding that will enable us to maintain our friendship.

When I asked to stay here until I was well enough to drive home, I was unsure if you would let me. While you have left the Catholic Church, I know the Church has not left you. That you let me stay means you really do love me, albeit with your silence and conditions. Although your silence and conditions have hurt me, I understand why you need them, and I deeply thank you and love you for this.

I know you find it hard to understand how a physician's wife becomes "accidentally" pregnant. But then, isn't that a bit like wondering how a priest "accidentally" becomes an alcoholic on altar wine? If God didn't want to weed out who She welcomes into Heaven, She would have skipped making Earth, and made all Her creatures perfect.

Rick and I have always used condoms (even when I was on the Pill). Although I've taken the HIV antibody test and come out negative enough times to feel pretty certain my past isn't going to catch up with me, Rick's job as a surgeon puts him at a slight risk of being infected with the virus. Two years ago, I stopped taking the Pill. (After being on it for sixteen years, my body rebelled.) Because Rick and I rarely have sex, and because no condom failed in the four years in which we used them, I didn't bother to get fitted for a diaphragm, or to buy spermicide. Trust me, I now know that just because something works for years, it doesn't mean it'll always work. Condoms can, and do, break. (And, as anxious as I was during the minutes I had to wait to see if I had tested positive with my home pregnancy test kit, it was nothing when compared to the anxiety Rick and I felt for days when we waited to learn if we tested HIV-positive.)

During the time I've been here, Kip has been such a dear to me. Each time he brings me home a frozen yogurt or some other treat, and sits and talks to me, I thank God that he's been willing to be deceived about the nature of my surgery. My abortion would only cause him pain. In some ways, he would feel more betrayed by my actions than Rick.

When Portia became "accidentally" pregnant with her fourth child, Hunter spent the better part of a Sunday in her room, and pleaded with her to keep their child. Finally, in a desperate move, he called their three children into Portia's bedroom. As we stood with our backs against the wall, he asked each of us if Portia should abort the child. The vote was tied, with Hunter and Grace voting "no" for the abortion (back then, Grace either didn't respond or said "no" to everything), and Portia and I voting "yes." At the age of seven and a half Kip followed my lead, as he has always done, and cast the deciding "yes."

Given the instability of our home, and Grace's challenge; given the facts that by then Portia was twenty-one years into her daily speed habit and that the fetus would, at some point in childhood, become a depository for their uncles' sperm, Portia's rage, and Hunter's indifference, it seemed that this choice was an instance in which a delicate sliver of good peels from the trunk of a rotted tree.

Unlike "true believers" such as yourself, I don't think God, Our Mother, would choose, much less want, the existence that Kip and Grace and I had for yet another of

Her unborn children. I also think She understands that simple solutions that readily separate black from white do not allow for the multi-hues that shade the more complex issues found in lives that must be lived one hour at a time to be survived. (And survive is barely what one can do in a family in which the majority of its members have created, for generations, the outward illusion of an ordinary and loving family with the tools of silence and deceit.) Like twins, incest has occurred in our family for generations.

I don't remember much about my maternal great-grandfather, Grandpa Bing, except that he had always seemed old and mean. Portia's brothers said he hadn't always been mean. The cruelty came after his return from the ten years he spent locked away in "the hospital," deprived of the company of his friends and family for a disease with a name and symptoms that neither his wife, or children, or grandchildren could manage to ever remember. It was after his release that Grandpa Bing began to corner and rape his grandsons.

This violence became a mite that ate into our family tree, cracking its limbs and disfiguring the fruit of each generation. Soon, Grandpa Bing's eldest grandson turned on his twin sister, Portia, cornering and raping her when she was sixteen, and planting the mite's seed in her being. Fifteen years later, Portia and the survivors of her generation turned on my siblings and me on numerous occasions.

In my life there won't be an hour, a minute, or a second of a day in which I won't be disfigured by the madness that unites me to Portia, her pedophiliac brothers, and the abusive relatives who precede us. But unlike Portia and her brothers, I acknowledge that this madness may allow the catastrophe of rape and abuse to control, and thereby destroy, my life and any life that might flow from me. I accept that I am unable to look a child in the eye and say, with 100-percent certainty, "I'll never molest you, I'll never emotionally batter you, or lock you in the closet for the day." Had I been born in another time, in which pregnancy was not a choice — well, let's just say another few twigs on the family tree would have been destroyed. Therapy at best provides understanding, acceptance, and forgiveness; on rare occasions it works miracles. But I sadly must accept that I was not such an occasion, and therefore, I never want to have children.

But that's not why I didn't give up for adoption the child I aborted today. I aborted the child because of Grace. I could trust strangers to love and care for a healthy child, but I couldn't trust strangers to love and care for a challenged one. And who can guess what challenge might present itself in the second generation after Portia's addiction to speed?

I struggled for weeks with whether or not I should tell Rick that we had conceived a child. I pictured buying maternity clothes, going to Lamaze classes, and giving birth to our infant. But I knew that after I gave birth I would have to abandon Rick and our child. And I couldn't abandon a baby to a parent who would always be absent. A child is not an oversized terrier who can be left alone in the yard with a pile of chew toys and a stack of biscuits while it waits for its master to come out and play at its master's convenience. And it would be all the more cruel to give such a life to a child who comes into this world challenged.

Twice in my life I've voted for death. I don't have it within me to take this vote again. Accordingly, I chose to be sterilized. This may not be the step that others in my position would take, but for me, it was the only choice I had, given my view of life's most muted shades of gray. I can only hope and pray that because you also recognize that life is composed of a multitude of grays, you will be able to understand my reasons behind my difficult choice and, once again, unconditionally love me.

I know. You're trying to piece together the whole of this picture, a picture that includes snapshots of Molly-my-magnificent, Molly-the-companion-Carolyn-needs, Molly-your-mangy (yes, my ears have tuned into your whispered curses). But you see, my family's old double standard, which demanded that we allow our madness to roam free only in the safety of our own households, only compels me to destroy my own offspring. And for this, I am thankful, because it permits me to have a caring relationship with another person's loving child.

Please understand that these times are hard for me. For eternity my soul will be gouged by what I did. But I don't think that you would have brought me into your home and cared for me as you have unless you believed our relationship allowed for us to make choices that are so very different. It is for this freedom of choice that I most thank, and love, you.

Carolyn

P.S. As for our country's present hysteria over incest and child sexual abuse, well, let's just say I think it's become the Salem witch-hunt of our twenty-first century. And like all witch-hunts, no good will come from it. Granted, the media has performed admirably in proving that incest and sexual abuse are common enough to no longer be labeled "abnormal" behavior. (How can anything be abnormal that happens with such frequency?) Now it's time to move to the next step. We must aid the abused, and the abusers, in seeking the means by which they will be healed, so that similar harm won't befall our nation's next generation. If the federal government would use the funds earmarked for two or three F-22 fighter planes to improve access to mental health care — oops, sorry — I think I may have accidentally taken too much pain medication.

December 13

Dear Diary,

I just read Carolyn's letter. I feel for her. I had no idea how deep and how lasting her scars were. It really saddens me. But it also gives me this feeling in the pit of my stomach, like I used to get in grade school when I was waiting to get back a spelling test I knew I hadn't done well on.

I don't know why this would frighten me. Oh, well, I think I'll send her some flowers.

Ruby

FTD WIRE

December 13

Dear Carolyn,

Sometimes flowers say what we cannot. Good luck, and I am touched by your courage and your honesty. Where I am touched is not important ... only kidding.

Ruby Rae

December 14

Dear Ruby Rae,

Why do I have sudden cravings for pork rinds, Big Macs, and whiskey? (Jack Daniels Green, no less.) I swear to the Almighty that on my drive home from L.A., I had — absolutely had — to pull into a truck stop on Interstate 5 just below "the grapevine." (If you ever need anything transported by a big-rig, just let me know.)

The name on the truck stop's sign was "Boomer's House of Beef, Babes, & Billiards." Needless to say, it's the first time I've ever been near a pool table that wasn't in the game room of a private residence. (I won't even go into what I said to the first man who called me "Babe." But afterwards, he thanked me for giving him your phone number.) I guess, after all those days of staying with you, the smell of the establishment's barbecued ribs and greasy french fries just pulled me in from the highway.

It will please you to know I loaded up on two (non-alcoholic) Lime Rickies, four double packs of Hostess Twinkies (I'd never had one. Pretty tasteless, but lots of sugar and fat, which reminded me of you), and a side of barbecued chicken that had cooked in one of those glassed-in rotisseries for at least a week. After I got back on the road, my stomach puffed right up until it was the size of a cantaloupe (I attributed this to the Lime Rickies, which I drank rather quickly after the salty french fries). I considered pulling off the road. But the thought of splurging and then purging was just too, too you. Thank God there's a limit to how much of you can rub off on me.

When I got home, I found my letter that you sent back with the message "Return to sender, addressee in no mood." Rick didn't even ask me about the comment. (If men were at least curious, they'd make for much more interesting and involved companions.) In fact, Rick wasn't even home. This deeply disappointed me after what he had said to me in our last few phone conversations. As usual, there was a note on the fridge. I didn't have to read it to know he'd been called to the hospital for an emergency surgery.

When I went into our bedroom, I found your flowers on my nightstand. There's nothing nicer to find in a bedroom than a beautiful arrangement of flowers — unless, of course, you count finding a naked man or the latest issue of *Playgirl*. (Rick's always been rather fond of finding the Frederick's of Hollywood catalogue on his nightstand. Personally, I don't see the point. I mean, if you want to look at women, why not look in *Playboy* or *Oui?* I swear if lesbians didn't spend so much time in bed talking about giving up perfume to be politically correct, I'd be willing to give up men. But then, technically, I may have already done that. I mean, for the past few years it seems like I've always taken care of my own needs, if you know what I mean.)

Anyway, Rick came home five hours later. He mumbled something about a drunken man who oversteered his car, and drove it off a cliff. The guy's wife flipped out when Rick told her that her husband would never walk again. She said she would close all of their bank accounts, take their four kids out of state, and divorce her husband.

After standing on his feet for the six-hour surgery, and then spending an hour trying to calm his patient's livid wife, Rick was too tired to even care I was home, much less that I was in the same bed as him. In light of my recent surgery, I suppose this was for the best.

I lay in bed unable to sleep. I listened to Rick's even breathing. That's when I realized it's not that he doesn't love me, he's just too damned tired to show me. I'm certain that's all it is. If he didn't care for me, he wouldn't have phoned me every day when I was at your house. If he didn't care, I would know this in my heart, and my heart wouldn't have allowed me to come back here. Well, maybe that's not completely true.

If I hadn't come home, I would have had to face running into more of nothing. Running into nothing, when I am all alone, frightens me more than anything else in the world.

It's only when I'm home with my husband that I can face the nothingness that's out there in the world.

Anyway, thank you again for all you did for me in L.A. I'm deeply touched you were willing to wade beside me through my shades of gray. And, to show my appreciation, I'd like more than anything to make a donation in your name to the convent where you were a novitiate. If you don't have time to send me the address before you and Kip drive up for Christmas, I'll remember to ask you for it when you're here.

So, what day will you arrive with Kip and Grace? The twenty-third would be great, but the twenty-second would be even better. It'll give us lots of time to make a gingerbread house, string popcorn and cranberries, and do some caroling! (Molly loves caroling.) And we'll definitely do midnight mass! By the way, does your family open presents on Christmas Day, or Eve? (Please say day!)

Well, I'm off to pick up Molly. She's going to help me cut down a Christmas tree. Afterwards, we'll bake gingerbread people. Since my surgery, my attachment to her has grown even stronger. (That dreadful Olga is so unreasonably strict, it's no wonder that Molly prefers to be with me after school.) If only I had been blessed with the strength needed to hack down the madness from my childhood. Then I could have had my very own Molly! Imagine what my life would have been like if I could have been a mother, a real mother, to my very own children. Life can feel so cold and cruel at Christmas.

Carolyn

P.S. Would you be a Christmas angel and make a little detour on your way up here? Well, okay, it's more than just a little detour. But I wouldn't ask the favor if you weren't my best friend, and closest sister. I need you to make a little stop in San Diego. Specifically, at Sea World. Molly's absolutely crushed because her mother didn't bring her home a giant, stuffed Shamu the Whale when she went down there on a recent business trip. As it is, poor Molly so hates it when Meg goes away on business. (And you'd think that knowing that, Meg would have the good sense to bring her only child a present. I mean, it's bad enough that Meg found Molly's father in some tube in a sperm bank.)

Anyhow, when I phoned down to have a Shamu sent to me by U.P.S., they said it wouldn't arrive by Christmas — and Molly has to have it for Christmas! The right present can be so important to a five-year-old. So, will you be a sweetie, and put some magic in a precious child's Christmas?

December 18

Dear Diary,

First of all, I'm standing at the edge of my grave, and what's dripping from my lips? Lies ... lies to Rick for Carolyn, I can't believe this. And if this isn't bad enough, Carolyn wants to get in touch with my old convent. More lies! The last thing I need is Carolyn setting up a line of communication with the nuns. The thought of her on the phone to Mother Mary Timothy! It's bad enough being on the verge of dying and going to hell without also being dragged into public disgrace on the way down. If she gets in contact with my old convent ... they'll have to hire people to go to my funeral.

I feel like a constipated yak. Don't ask me why, I just do. I have the flux, honey ... the pre-purgatory-possibly-hell flux. Funny, I never thought about purgatory until I got this tumor, or whatever it is I got.

I can't go up there for Christmas, because I'll have to tell one lie after the other ... and I could drop dead any minute, and with a mortal sin on my soul ... flames ... high, hot, heavy, and steady. I'm talking the big hibachi. On the other hand, I'd have to come up with a good lie, or kill Carolyn, not to go up there for Christmas. Not to mention, I'm five seconds away from breaking Molly's neck and yet another commandment ... if she drags one more empty booze bottle or added pound into the light.

You know, the way I'm gaining weight, my tumor could be registering beyond the scan. I think I better call Dr. Hickman ... but before I do that, I've got to put the kibosh on Christmas, and I know just how to do it.

Through the teeth and over the tongue, look out stomach here it comes...

Ruby Rae

EXPRESS MAIL

December 18

Dear Carolyn,

How dare you order me to go to Sea World and pick up a Shamu for that little snotty-nosed, peanut-butter-breathed brat next door to you? Live your mother fantasy on your own time ... and energy, I might add. San Diego is a hundred miles in the wrong direction ... and that's a hundred miles one way ... screw you very much.

If her mother didn't get her a Shamu, then she obviously doesn't need one. There are some things in this world that you can't control, or haven't you learned that? You're such a control freak, Carolyn. It's one of your worst flaws. Anyway, I'm annoyed. I'm put out, and I don't feel like spending Christmas with you and that snaggletoothed Heidi from hell. You have a lot of nerve just assuming that I'll do this and that for you. I'm your sister-in-law, I'm not on your household staff. So Christmas is off ... got it? Christmas, Easter, St. Patrick's Day, Thanksgiving, Yom Kippur, Ramadan, Labor Day, Bastille Day, Passover, Hanukkah, All Souls' Day, Veterans Day, Cinco de Mayo, Fourth of July, and any other holiday ... they're all off. I need some space. I've been violated ... and part of my liberation is to not allow myself to be oppressed by anyone ... even a fellow oppressee! So don't call me, I'll call you. And don't hold your breath. Better yet ... do hold your breath.

Ruby Rae

December 18

Dear Diary,

I'm back again. I just wrote the last scathing letter to Carolyn. She should be livid with me for weeks. Of course, now I'll need a story to tell Kip why we're not going to Carolyn's for Christmas. He'll be pissed off. He loves going to Carolyn's. It's no wonder ... "Oh, baby Kip ... look what I got for you..." She spoils the hell out of him. Then, it's always two weeks of "Carolyn does it this way..." when we get back. It's too bad Carolyn doesn't do everything I do ... then he wouldn't need me at all. Speaking of which, I know just what little lie to tell Kip.

Ruby

December 18

Dear Ruby Rae,

I'm so thrilled! I just finished my short story! I did everything you said to do to tighten it up. Since I think you'll love it, I've taken the liberty of enclosing a dozen copies: one for you and one for your agent, and ten for all of your writer friends.

Also, I spoke to Professor Glendower, who heads the writers' group at the university. She read my material, and said I've been accepted into the group. She thinks that with just a bit of work, my novel will be ready to market. Isn't life heavenly? It's so terrific that everything's happening at my very favorite time of year! (If only I didn't have all this year-end work for Rick's office. Then I could bake cookies and fudge during the rest of the day!)

Only one more thing is needed to make my life picture-perfect for Christmas: Rick. If he would take off a weekend, or even a night, to be alone with me — oh, it would be so perfect! I've asked him twice for "a date" on this Saturday night, but as usual, no response. I'd ask a third time, but that seems to border on begging. The only begging I accept at Christmas is the kind you see standing in front of Macy's wearing a Santa Claus suit and ringing a bell for the Salvation Army. And since a Santa suit looks terrible on me, I'm not going to ring any bells, or beg.

Since my surgery, I so need to be held, to be assured I'm still a good, and lovable, and desirable person. Oh, well, at least Molly wants me. If I were a bad person, a child wouldn't reach out to me. Children are too pure and honest to want or love a bad person.

Looking forward to seeing you in a few days. Your company will light up my life like a Christmas tree.

I love you,
Carolyn

P.S. While Rick's at a meeting tonight, I'm going to start on another short story. God only knows what my life would be like if I didn't love my work!

VIA FEDERAL EXPRESS

December 21

Dear Grinch:

I just got your letter of the eighteenth, Mzzzz. Ruby Rae Rhinoceros! (And anything kind, or nice, or loving that I said in my letter of that same date is herewith canceled. I wouldn't want to see you even if you were the last stuffed Shamu in the gift shop at Sea World. So, don't try to worm yourself back into my good graces by shipping yourself up here in a U.P.S. truck.)

At first, I thought you must be the cruelest person the devil ever placed on the face of the earth. I remained in this mind frame until Rick was called into the hospital at four this morning. (Remember the wife of the drunk who drove his car off the cliff? Well, instead of draining her husband's bank account and taking the kids out of state, she slit her wrists. Rick had the task of splicing her veins together again.) After he left, I couldn't sleep, so I came downstairs. I made a cup of tea, and sat in my favorite chair.

For a while, I thought about the four children of the drunk and the suicide. When I realized I couldn't do anything for them but worry, I focused my thoughts on you. As the sun rose, I was struck by the thought that there's something more than mean-spiritedness and booze behind your recent, and most peculiar, behavior. Could it be fear? Have I gotten too close to a secret?

Trust me, I know all about letting out secrets. Once they're out, you have to deal with them. And that's very, very messy, and very, very scary. But dealing with them is soooo much easier than not dealing with them. If you don't believe me, look at what holding in secrets did for Portia.

It wasn't until the morning after Portia's death that her children learned she had been raped by her twin brother. At last we understood why she had spent the better part of her life popping pills, and living a life of lies that made her out to seem so grand. The secret in her heart had festered, and produced a wound that made her feel impure, inferior, and imperfect. To survive, Portia couldn't be who she was, so she created another self, and lived her life as this second self.

Once we knew her secret, we understood why she turned a deaf ear and blind eye to what had happened to us, as it happened to us back then. It wasn't that she didn't care we were raped. She lacked the ability to confront it and make her brothers accountable for their behavior toward us.

The part of Portia that enabled her to stand up for herself died on the day she was raped by her twin. As children, we turned to that part of her for protection, not knowing it no longer existed. Once we knew the truth, we stopped blaming her for not defending us. You cannot hold a parent responsible for giving what they do not have to give.

On the day after Portia's death, we realized her brothers had known she lacked the ability to protect us. So, while they may or may not have understood that they were sexually abusing us, while they may or may not have understood that sexual abuse is wrong, they knew that what they did to us would always be safe from prosecution. Or, to put it another way, Portia's children paid a high price for her lack of self-worth.

Knowing Portia's secret, I now understand that when she locked us in closets, and yelled through their doors that she hated us, she wasn't yelling at us. She was yelling at her secret. It was her secret, rather than us, that she shoved into a closet. Portia's tragedy wasn't that she did this to her children. Her tragedy was that she died without knowing her secret was the plastic wrap that covered her madness like a head of lettuce. She would only have had to remove this outer wrapping and her madness would have come apart in her hands.

But since she didn't know this, her funeral reception was in a mansion filled with antiques, and paintings, and china, and books that she had led her friends to believe she owned when she didn't. And all three of her pedophiliac brothers came, including her rapist. (In his mind, Portia's twin had made amends by sending Portia a new negligee each week during the months of her illness.) At the reception, I stood on the landing of Villa Adagio's double staircase and watched this man, this church-going rapist, eat the catered food provided by my father's line of credit. I saw him pat the hands of Portia's friends as they spoke of her in the pleasing images that she so painstakingly created in order to be accepted by them. As I watched this, I wondered what Portia's friends would have said had they known the brother who comforted them had been Portia's rapist? — What would any of these socialites have said had they known the room was also playing host to another two men who were in the habit of raping children, including a child who was born challenged?

As our next-door neighbor's grown daughter (who was one of Hunter's more recent ex-mistresses) offered me her condolences, I was trying to decide which of these revelations would cause our guests the most discomfort. Given their backgrounds, they'd probably have the most difficult time knowing they were eating food purchased with a line of credit. Portia and our rapes would have been brushed away as if they were bits of white lint on a black dress.

If Portia were beside me right now, she would say the saddest thing about her funeral reception was that it was held in a mansion she didn't own. Then I would have to tell her that wasn't the saddest thing at all. The saddest thing was that her funeral reception was attended by friends she didn't know. Portia's secret prevented her from feeling good enough about herself to take the risk of making one real friend in her lifetime. That she never had a single friend who knew the all of her, and loved her in spite of it, is the great tragedy of her life. Because without ever having a true friend, and without ever having been a true friend to herself, Portia died before she ever lived. Isn't it a shame the truth can't help the dead?

Of course, you're young and healthy (albeit a tad fluffy), so I realize you haven't any reason to be contemplating death. Nevertheless, it might be wise to take a minute and ask yourself: "If I die today, would I die before I've lived?" And if you answer yes, what is it that you haven't done, or said, or faced, that would cause you to die such an awful death?

Oh, and speaking of facing things, did I mention we have a friend in common? The good Sister Barbara Marie of the Little Sisters of Saint Jude. (Like you, she always had a weakness for St. Jude, the patron saint of lost causes.) And, yes, of course I have met Mother Mary Timothy! I can't believe it's taken me this long to put these two names together.

Barbara was in my class at Mount Carmel High School. And, like you, she went straight into the novitiate after graduation. As for Mother Timothy, we met when I visited Barbara at the novitiate. It's amazing our paths never crossed, isn't it? What year did you say you went in? '71, '72, '73? Or did you tell me?

You know, it just seems to me that everything was going along fine between us until I offered to make a donation to your old novitiate. I guess I'll just have to make my annual Christmas call to Sister Barbara Marie to learn about the secret you left behind the thick convent walls.

As for Christmas, well, you obviously aren't going to let Kip or Grace come up. So, I'm shipping a large care package to all of you. Molly is concerned about your health, so she gave me some nice sprouts for you. (She grew them herself in class.) Personally, I'm leaning toward sending you something in a whole-wheat grain. Or, better yet, I might mow the lawn, and send you the clippings! And don't you worry, I'll be sure to include a very small lump of coal for you.

Goodbye for now,
Carolyn

P.S. In view of your unlimited supply of creativity, you probably told Kip that Rick and I are rafting down the

Amazon for the holiday — I certainly hope you didn't say we flew to Brazil. It takes a dire emergency to get me up in the air. To me a plane is rather like a large walk-in closet that's being flown by Portia on a day she's run slightly short of speed and the hairdresser who supplies her refills is in Mexico for two weeks. Touché.

P.P.S. Oh, and about me living my "mother fantasies" through Molly? Well, darling, why do I need Molly for this when I have you?

P.P.P.S. Yes, I am a control junkie. (At least I can acknowledge my habit, unlike you, you Grinch who stole everyone's Christmas.) And strictly speaking from one junkie to another, it wouldn't hurt you a bit to visit the Betty Ford Clinic. You know, Palm Springs is lovely this time of year.

December 24

Dear Diary,

I feel like a hair net belonging to a headless woman ... totally worthless. I'm in trouble. Carolyn was smarter than I thought she was. She figured out that my little argument with her was just a ploy to avoid Christmas and the convent.

Even worse, she knows Sister Barbara Marie and Mother Mary Timothy! I'll be glad to get to purgatory after she talks to them. Well, first things first. I'm going to confession. Regardless of what happens with Carolyn and how much she finds out, I have to keep a clean soul at all times ... 'cause these fumes I'm smelling are getting stronger every day.

I need a drink and a slab of ribs. At a time like this, a girl needs to be drunk and greasy, but nooo ... I've got to avoid those seven deadly sins ... everything is a sin ... hell, I'm ready to die. Anyway, off to confession.

Ruby Rae

December 24

Dear Diary,

I just got back from confession. You won't believe this. I was in the confessional for almost two hours! And you know that created a huge back-up with the holiday rush. People looked at me when I came out like I'd just shot the Holy Father. Not only that, the priest refused to absolve me. He said I wasn't truly trying to repent. He said I was really just trying to alleviate a little guilt, and that my manipulation and hiding of facts about my life was ongoing. He said I must be willing to change and 'fess up before I could be absolved. Now what kind of way is that for a Jesuit priest to think? Especially since he's been hearing my confessions for years. What ever happened to the good old days when you just listed your sins like a grocery list and the priest reciprocated with a list of prayers? I wanted to rip that screen out and snatch the priest through the hole and choke my absolution out of him.

Well, fine! I guess I'll just throw myself on the mercy of Carolyn. I'll come clean. I'll tell her everything, but only for one reason — I can't stand a lot of heat.

Ruby Rae

VIA FEDERAL EXPRESS

December 24

Dear Carolyn,

Okay. All right. I did wrong. I'm sorry. I know you won't understand. But please don't drag Kip into this. You're right, I did want to avoid my old convent days. I'm sorry about Christmas. Tell me what you want me to do. I'll do anything ... just forgive me. You don't understand. Don't talk to Sister Barbara Marie about me. I'll tell you the whole sordid tale.

I was eighteen, and so was he. He had those big blue eyes that look up and down a girl like a searchlight, and curly black hair, and he was all muscley from doing lots of manual labor ... you see, he was the janitor's son. At night sometimes, when the other girls were studying, I'd meet him down by the grotto and we'd go for a walk through the cemetery and talk. Then he started sweet-talking me. He got me drunk on altar wine, and told me everything would be all right. I know. Sacrilege. The next thing I knew my breasts were bare and I was putting jalapeño Cheez Whiz on the sacred hosts. It gets blurry from that point on. All I remember is wanting to please, trying to please, and then waking up to a livid, shocked, and speechless Mother Mary Timothy with Sister Barbara Marie at her side. They had come into the chapel for their daily matins at four a.m. and found me and Steve passed out drunk on the altar, jalapeño Cheez Whiz and hosts everywhere, and to make matters worse, I had fallen asleep with his male part still in my mouth.

So I lied. So I didn't leave the religious order on my own accord. I was asked to leave. Even though I begged for forgiveness and a second chance. As Mother Mary Timothy said, "You have a calling in this life, dear ... but it's not religious."

Okay. So there you have it. I was kicked out of the convent for having sex on the altar and drinking altar wine and feeding jalapeño Cheez Whiz and hosts to the janitor's son. I just can't have Kip find this out. He thinks he was my first. Emotionally and spiritually and theoretically he was. Just like Rick, your fourth husband. Only I didn't need any alum. It's important to Kip to be the first. Don't crush him. He'll dump me if he finds out he's not the first and only.

I'm at your mercy. I know I've done you wrong. Please forgive me. Come on, even the Catholic Church forgives...

Ruby Rae

December 26

Dear Ruby Rae,

I am not the Catholic Church, so I'm not empowered to forgive. But, since you seem to think I am, I think I'll start out with the first thing the Mother Church gives before she doles out forgiveness. That's right: penance. And lots of it. Ready? Here it is: Winnifred Hernandez-Hirschschimer, my former therapist (soon you, too, will learn that her name barely fits on a check's "pay to order" line). Her office is in the Los Angeles Marina, and she specializes in drawing out secrets. Ugly little secrets that are deeper and darker than hors d'oeuvres of sacred hosts with jalapeño Cheez Whiz. (At Mount Carmel, we always used honey. Oh! The things we did with honey! — But then, you'd know all about honey, if you'd had more than two men. And speaking of men, just because I've had a few more husbands than you've had dates is no reason to mask your jealousy behind such righteousness!)

Anyway, the next time you aren't suffering from double vision from all that booze you drink, look up Winnifred in the phone directory, and make an appointment to see her. Then, drop me a line, and we'll talk forgiveness.

A very hurt, and somewhat still livid,
Carolyn

P.S. What's happening with my short story?

December 29

Dear Diary,

You've heard of Blue Monday, well, today was Black Friday. Carolyn is blackmailing me into seeing her old therapist. Why does everybody want me to see a therapist? I'm not crazy. I'm dying. Of course, Carolyn doesn't know that.

It's getting worse, too. The longer I stay sober, and on this diet, the stronger the smells of oil and gasoline get; the stronger the taste of blood.

I'm spacey too. I wander around in a daze, wondering where I'm going, when in fact I'm already there.

I've taken all of these tests, and still, no results. What do I have? And how did I get it?

Ruby Rae

December 30

Dear Mzzzz. Ruby Rae Scrooge,

Bah-humbug, and a lousy post-Xmas to you! First, I'm still livid. Second, guess who had a most unmerry Christmas? Of course, how could it be anything but that, after my favorite sister's personality split and, lo and behold! out came the Grinch? Next year I'll take the pagan route, and quietly celebrate the Winter Solstice.

On Christmas, Rick worked from ten a.m. to six p.m., and returned to the hospital at nine. (I guess when you think about it, his holiday was much worse than mine.) During the hours he was away from work, we went out for dinner. I was so disappointed, I could barely eat the main course, much less dessert. (And Chocolate Decadence has always been my favorite.)

When will I stop setting myself up for disappointments that come from craving the things I'll never get in my life, like the hugs and kisses and laughter and sharing I so wanted on Christmas? Three Lents ago, I gave up the fun that comes from exchanging gifts with Rick on birthdays, anniversaries, and Christmas, because he doesn't believe in presents. But hugs and kisses and sharing and laughter — does he not believe in them? Apparently not. In order to preserve what's left of my sanity, I'd best make a New Year's resolution to give up wanting them.

On top of this, my plans for Molly fizzled. You were right about Shamu the Whale. Well, sort of right. Meg gave Molly a Shamu for Christmas. She also took her away on Christmas Eve for a surprise, week-long trip to Yosemite. Molly was full of smiles when she dashed over here for her gifts before they left. She said she and her mom were going to have the "bestest time" in the park's beginners' ski classes.

I wanted her to open my presents before she ran home to pack. I had so looked forward to the thrill of watching her pull off the ribbons and wrapping. But she wanted to save them for Christmas morning.

When I went over to feed her fish, Wilbur and Mr. Ed (Olga somehow managed to land a man, Horatio Elgar, III. They spent the holiday climbing rocks in the desert), my still-wrapped gifts were on the kitchen counter. I was crushed. I so wanted Molly to have the hand-knitted Christmas sweater with the matching mittens and hat on the holiday. She told me she needed this more than anything after a classmate came to school wearing the wool holiday look. As for the book, *Anne of Green Gables,* and the heart-shaped locket with the diamond chip, they could wait to be opened until she returned. Still, it hurt me that she didn't want to take them with her. Maybe she wanted to, but Meg wouldn't let her. I'll try to ask Molly about this once she's home.

Molly's absence has highlighted the fact that Rick is no different than any of my other husbands. He's simply not there. Even when he's home with me, he's not here, or at least he's not here with me. I know his work is stressful, but then, so is a relationship that no longer works.

Maybe if we had had a honeymoon — maybe if Rick was willing to go on vacation, or at least take off a weekend — maybe if ... Lately, when I think of Rick, I find myself whispering, "Maybe if..." Then pride silences my tongue so that others won't share in my painful knowledge that I've again set up housekeeping in another lonely marriage.

Whenever I think about my abortion, and making the difficult decision to be sterilized, I find myself asking, is anyone out there taking care of Carolyn besides Carolyn? No. Carolyn is the only person who even knows that Carolyn is alive; that Carolyn has needs; that Carolyn feels pain. Carolyn's the only person who knows a part of her died after her surgeries. It's very strange, and very lonely, to sleep beside a man who is oblivious to this. But then, for all I know a part of Rick may also be dead. Perhaps I've just been too wrapped up in myself to be aware of it.

One thing is for certain, if I keep this up the Calvin in me will revert back to Catholic and you'll see me dressing in grim Mary Martyr. And the sackcloth look has never done a thing for me. In light of this, maybe I should consider making a different New Year's resolution than giving up hugs and kisses and sharing and laughter. Yes! That's what I'll do! I'll find myself a brand-new lap to lay my heart in. — It's time for me to take out a relationship ad. Just imagine, a brand-new husband! It's the perfect New Year's gift for me!

Carolyn

January 2

Dear Diary,

I just got back from seeing Winnifred. It was different. It wasn't that bad. I kinda enjoyed it. She says everything I say to her is safe ... and I believe her.

I told her about the smells and the tumor, and that it doesn't show up on the scans. She says she has her "suspicions" about the tumor, and asked me if it "had to be a tumor." I felt relieved talking to her.

I really liked it. I've decided to go twice a week.

Ruby Rae

January 14

Dear Diary,

I just got back from seeing Winnie. She had my medical records ... including my many scans. She's convinced I don't have a tumor. She says she's not certain what I do have, but she's "curious."

She said she didn't want to talk about the smells and tastes right now. She wanted to talk about my childhood. Funny, I don't remember anything before nine. She says that's "curious."

Ruby Rae

January 14

Dear Carolyn,

First of all, thank you for turning me on to Winnifred. I've been four times and I call her Winnie. I'm learning a lot about myself.

I'm sorry things were so bad with Molly at Christmas, but you need to go on. You're not her mother and even if you were, she would walk out of your life someday, just like it was bath time.

I think the issue here for you is to accept the fact that you are childless and always will be, not to fill your life with surrogate children. Your need to do this makes me "curious."

Anyway, you're not alone. It just feels like that now. You'll be okay. It'll be okay. Just you wait and see. You call me if you need me. You know I'm open all night.

I don't feel much like writing. I think I'll go and take a walk on the beach. I need the air. I need to look out and not see land.

Take care,
Ruby Rae

P.S. Sorry about everything I put you through. But you don't know the half of it. Right now, I can't talk about it. Just please believe me, I'm sorry about Christmas, and for the record ... mine was miserable, too. Kip's old USC buddies dropped in, and I felt fat, and obligated to serve them.

You know what's funny? Kip is around me all the time, and I still feel sad and lonely.

January 17

Ruby Rae,

"Curious," are we? Yep, you've seen Winnifred. (As for nicknames: when I was dealing with my issues with men, it made it very convenient to be able to call her "Fred.") I guess as Kip's post-Christmas gift, you decided to sober up. (Why else would your penmanship be neater, as well as your "thought process," if you can call it that?)

As for Molly, well, I know you've never much liked her. So, when I read your little "curious" comment, I tried to divorce myself from this. My decision to be childless was not an easy decision. It was the right decision. And just because it was right, it doesn't make this aspect of my life any less dark. — I hate to break this news to you, but you haven't cornered the market on sad and lonely times. Why don't you reread some of my old letters some time. (Or don't you keep them?)

Carolyn

P.S. And speaking of dark, I've begun writing a relationship ad. I thought I'd place it in one of those free, weekend-activity papers. You know, just to test the water — just to see what other fish are in the pond. Pretty desperate, huh? Oh, well, as they always say, it's darkest before the dawn.

P.P.S. Have you even read my short story? If you don't think it's good, just tell me.

January 19

Dear Diary,

This is it. I can't go on. All day long, I smell oil and gasoline. I taste blood. I've been to three dentists, my teeth are in great shape and my gums aren't bleeding.

Am I crazy? Am I like that madman that sits in the park cursing dive-bombers that aren't there? Virginia Woolf was an author and she threw herself into a river. That would qualify as crazy. So obviously being published and respected professionally does not save you from being crazy.

I want a Big Mac. A Big Mac, a Quarter Pounder with Cheese, six orders of fries, and a gallon of Jim Beam. I don't know why ... I just do. But I can't. I've got to keep my soul and slate clean for that minute when I cross the River Styx ... knowing my luck, I'll have to swim.

Ruby

January 21

Dear Carolyn,

I'm sorry things are so bad for you up there on the lake. However, let me tell you something ... running off to another man, like Catfyshe always did, is not going to solve your problems. Sometimes I can't help but think that loneliness is not so much a lack of company as it is an absence of kind.

I don't mean to get on your case ... but, please, you know the definition of insanity is trying the same thing over and over again and expecting a different outcome. I wish you and Catfyshe would learn that.

I gotta tell you, my image of you looking out of that window, all alone in the dark, in the mood for a man ... takes me back to Slag Alley ... and I don't want to see you in that light. Please don't do that to yourself. Don't do that to me.

You know, I still can't remember a thing before I was nine. How come? Am I crazy? When I ask Winnie she just says, "I'm curious about this" ... "I wonder if" ... "I can imagine" ... "Would it be okay if you were?" ... "Would it be okay if you weren't?" I wonder.

Winnie also says there is a good reason why I can't remember, and in time I will be able to remember what happened to me before I was nine. She thinks it might hold the key to the mystery of the smell of the oil and the gasoline.

You'd think, now that I'm seeing Winnie three times a week, she'd invest in decent pair of pumps ... honey, those chunk-heeled sling-backs!

Gotta go,
Ruby Rae

February 1

Dear R.R.,

Dear God! Not those chunk-heeled, sling-back shoes? Tell me they're not navy blue and don't sag in the middle! Those shoes were old six years ago — thank God they can't talk!

As for the other things you wrote about therapy — well, we'd better start at the top. First, you need to know a thing or three about therapists. They frequently say things like: "I find that rather curious" and "I wonder if" and "I can imagine." It's been my experience they use these phrases with greater frequency when they're bored, or when you've had the misfortune to be scheduled on a Friday afternoon. By then, they've had their fill of sob stories, and have heard at least ten tales that week that are far sadder than yours (and they have to bite their tongue to keep from telling you so).

If you consider it, there are but a few basic tales of woe. What makes them interesting, what gives them zest and keeps therapists awake during sessions, is the way people cope with whatever dysfunctional behaviors or situations they come up against. I came to think of Winnifred's "I wonder if"s, etc., and her long, searching look (which only those in her profession know how to give) as her kind way of moving me toward the chase scene, so I could keep down the cost of my monthly tab.

As for being crazy, don't let that bother you one bit. We're all mad to some degree. It's just that some of us are more honest and open about our "mad days." I've been crazy for years, and I've yet to let it bother me. Perhaps my writing is a release that enables my insanity to be more sane.

I think Winnifred hit the nail on the head about you blocking out events before the age of nine. Most people recall much younger memories. So when she says she thinks it's "curious" you can't remember, she's really saying you need to sort out why you choose not to remember.

As for your remarks about Catfyshe and me, might I suggest that on your next visit with your pal "Winnie" you ask her about "displaced anger"?

Off to Little Italy,
Carolyn

P.S. Oh, and speaking of Little Italy, here's a copy of my relationship ad. Don't you just love it? As for the potential for scandal, I'll place it in the weekly paper that comes out in the City. Well, it's partly to avoid scandal and partly because Rick is accustomed to me staying overnight in San Francisco when I go up to see a play or a ballet on the weekends. Besides, the men in San Francisco are just, well, so deliciously sophisticated on so many different levels. Oh! I can't wait for the basket the Easter Bunny brings me.

> SURGEON'S WIFE URGENTLY SEEKS one healthy, unattached man for weekend extravaganzas that can lead to anything mutually satisfying. You are sensitive and caring, and come equipped with knowledgeable and experienced hands. You may be any size, color, or shape, but don't look older than forty-five. N/S, N/D, no sickos or sports fans. Light S&M okay. As for me, I'm the everything you've ever dreamed of, and more. Your photo and letter get mine.

February 5

Dear Carolyn,

Light S&M? Please, that's like saying something is somewhat sugar-free. I can't believe you're doing this ... but I'm in too good a mood to get bothered by your silliness.

I had a great workout today! It seems like a new year. I ran into a bunch of NAPs (Negro American Princesses) on their way to their tennis lessons at the health club. You know those uppity black bitches that strut around acting like they're tan Jews. But even them and their Cheetos-colored hair, green designer contacts, and prettier-than-thou attitude couldn't destroy my resurgence of spirit. I'm back in the game. It's voondahbah, dah'ling. Even when my old beat-up Mercedes wouldn't go into reverse and I had to push it out of the parking space in front of those bitches, it didn't bother me one bit. The thought of running to McDonald's, or a cigarette, or a bar didn't cross my mind. I'm back in control!

Viva Jane Fonda, Hail Helen Reddy,
Ruby Rae

February 5

Dear Diary,

I just wrote the biggest letter full of lies to Carolyn. I had to. She needed cheering up. I'm in the grips of grief. I'm afraid to leave my house. I get lost on the way to the bathroom sometimes, and I keep having these blurry flashes. I tried. I swear I did, but I just couldn't be good anymore. I had to break some commandments.

The smell of oil and gasoline is so pungent I had to fry some chicken and I ate it all. I fried some more and ate that too. I know ... the seven deadly sins ... I don't care ... at this point, I'm obviously going to hell, so it might as well be with a smile on my face, and some chicken grease on my lips.

I also spent the afternoon with Jack, Jack Daniels, that is. It had been a long time. Too long. He missed me ... and I missed him. When I showed up at Winnifred's, she said I was drunk. She asked if I thought that I might be "an alcoholic," and if I'd ever been to AA. I asked her if she had ever been stabbed in the forehead by a client before.

She said the next time I had the urge to drink, I should consider something more constructive, like going to the gym. And so I shall. I'll go right on over to the Jim ... to the Jim Beamster. Here's mud in your eye...

Ruby Rae

February 6

Dear Diary,

I know this will be hard to read. My hand is shaking. I woke up this morning and I thought I was in the promised land. The wrong promised land. Fortunately, I had only fallen asleep face down in a large ashtray. But I gotta tell you, the smell of those ashes have set me straight.

Not to mention I spent all morning with my head in the toilet, and I had "the trots," as Carolyn would say. As Catfyshe would say, I "shit and puked up a breeze." It's not easy being a switch reliever. Ohhh, God. I gotta get to confession. I hope I don't die on the way. My tumor is really acting up today. I don't care what anybody says, I have a brain tumor ... at least one. I'll write more later.

Dear Diary,

I promised I'd write more later and it's later. Oh, what a day! My car was running low on gas on the way to the church. I tried to pump my own gas but I couldn't. The smell of it sent me off into hallucinations. I swear I saw Nikita Khrushchev having sex with Mamie Eisenhower. But that's not the worst of it. I ran out of gas on the freeway ... in a terrible neighborhood. So I decided to go to confession in a downtown slum church. I was desperate. I went into the confessional, and a wino opened up the screen and asked me if there was any paper on my side. Needless to say, I'd thrown up all over the place.

February 14

Ruby Rae!

Happy Valentine's Day! I just adore a day when you can all but taste the wispy scents of cinnamon-red-hot love on the air! You pushed your Mercedes out of a parking space? By yourself? With your four-inch-long fingernails? Did you come across one of Portia's old purses with a large stash of speed? Oh, well, if your next book doesn't sell, you can get work at a towing company. Your look is so well suited to a truck's cab.

As for me, I've had the most stupendous day! The holiday blahs and postoperative blues have been chased from my life. Being alive is just too, too fabu! No, I haven't finished my book. It's almost done, but I'm not happy over an "almost." I'm happy because today, I fell in sudden lust. (What can I say? St. Valentine is my patron saint!)

Anyway, I was on my way home from placing my relationship ad when I happened upon the most delightful detour that took me down Rose Street in the City. When I stopped to let a pedestrian cross, I looked to my right and saw this precious shop that sells antique lighting and custom drapery. The fabric in the window looked most chic, so I had to go in for Molly's sake. (Do you remember me mentioning the horrid girl in her kindergarten class who pranced about in her wool Christmas sweater with the matching mittens and cap? Well, her mother paid an interior decorator to redo her dollhouse. This dreadful child reduced Molly to tears by telling her she was cheap Christmas trash because Meg couldn't afford to give her a well-appointed dollhouse.)

I parked and dashed into Queen Anne's Lighting & Lace, Ltd., to look for fabric to sew into matching drapes and slipcovers for the windows and furniture in Molly's dollhouse. But the minute I entered the store — well, how shall I describe it? — Let's just say if I was Catfyshe, she would have just landed in Little Italy, and come up grinning with something other than linguine in her mouth.

That's right, Ruby Rae, I found a man. A fantastic man! He makes this month's *Playgirl* centerfold look as appealing as creamed corn and cubed steak. The instant my eyes spied him, they developed a mind of their own, and fingered his torso's richly grained textures. Minutes later, I realized he's also playful, and kind — and well, okay — maybe, just a smidgen gay. (But that's okay. Some lust-objects are all the more enjoyable when I know they're trés safe.)

Not to worry, Ruby Rae. The feminist in me is still saddened by the beauty cult in the gay community. But there are times when personal growth comes from experiencing life's other perspectives. And this, Ruby Rae, was one of those times. Because, honey, that too-gorgeous shop owner, Bruce, and Shawn, his adorable partner (who has an art studio adjacent to the store), were not to be ignored as they moved between bolts of imported fabric in their bare, well-muscled chests and short shorts under the heat from the very flattering lighting in their store. As I watched them, I thanked the Lord for this unseasonable heat wave, as well as California's laid-back atmosphere. Without this winning combination, there wouldn't have been any short shorts or bare chests for me to see today. (Or the need for me to spend some private time with my new issue of *Playgirl* the instant I got home.)

Well!!!! Between enjoying their too-wonderful physiques, and the stunning fabric, it's a wonder I ever made a selection. But an hour later, I did. And then, much to my surprise, Bruce gave me the fabric! Of course, it only amounted to a third of a yard, but still, with the thread and everything the purchase came close to twelve dollars. Naturally, he wouldn't have done this had I not told him about Molly-the-delightful, and my plans for her dollhouse. Doesn't your heart just melt around men who are kind to children and animals? (I should have mentioned this in my relationship ad.)

After the fabric and thread were bagged, Bruce and I chatted a bit, and I commented on the professional gas range in the kitchen at the back of his store. Minutes later, I struck a deal to give him a lesson on baking challah bread in return for the free fabric and thread. (You may have written the cookbooks, but do remember, dear, I am the family member who wins blue ribbons at the county fairs for my wonderful cakes and breads.) Needless to say, my offer pleased him. He said it'd be fun; as we baked, he might toss flour in my hair.

With those words, his playful nature tickled against my soul, and a deep hunger was begat. It was a yearning rooted in a deeper need than the lust that came to me after my eyes enjoyed the all of him. My gut urged me to run full-speed ahead, toss up sacks of flour, and then, perhaps, be hugged by that man. Fortunately, my pride stepped in and beat back that carefree feeling until it had no sensation, and was just another cold spot in my being.

Damn! Suddenly I wish I'd never met this delightful shop owner. If I hadn't, I wouldn't now sit with my back against another marriage that feels colder and emptier than any of my past marriages. Granted, I've felt alone while living with Rick for some time, but until now, this aloneness wasn't a feeling that ran such a deep course through the center of my being. What if no other man ever wants me? What if no one answers my relationship ad? I don't want to feel like this for the rest of my life. This aloneness walks me too near the edge of my madness. It's so frightening when my soul takes an unexpected dive. God only knows where I'll land.

Help me,
Carolyn

February 20

Dear Diary,

If this just don't take the paint off the barn. Carolyn's chasing a gay man. Here I am trying to die in peace and this girl just won't give me a peaceful moment. What is she doing? I'm going to ignore this. You know, if I hadn't "borrowed" the remainder of Hunter's liquid morphine, I'd think the girl had been dipping in it.

I'll write her a letter later. I gotta go to therapy. I tried to cancel, but Winnie said she was going to charge me anyway ... and that she was "curious" why I was trying to run away from therapy at this point. Maybe she's right when she says that when you don't want to go to therapy is when you need to be there the most.

Ruby Rae

February 20

Dear Carolyn,

I just got back from therapy. I remembered the road today. The road when I was five years old. It was a gravel country road in Michigan that ran between acres and acres of orchards. My father stopped the car and asked me who I liked better, him or Mamma. That was a big deal to them, who I liked better. Funny, I had forgotten that. They used to ask me that all the time when I was really little, like four or five, until that day on the road. As usual, I told them that I liked them both the same. But Daddy said that I had to like one of them better and if one of them had to die, which one would I choose? Then they asked if they got a divorce, who would I go with? I insisted I loved them the same.

Then they made me get out of the car and they drove off. And I was so scared that they weren't coming back. It was getting dark on the road and I didn't know exactly where I was, or how to get back home. I was afraid I'd be eaten by a wolf. (In Michigan there are vast forests and fields, and wolves roam in large packs and kill people all the time.)

Well, my parents came back. And they asked me again who I liked the best. They told me if I didn't tell them, they'd leave me forever, and if I didn't tell them the truth they'd know it. So, I told them Mamma. And then Daddy fell onto the steering wheel crying, and Mamma refused to look at me. And I felt so bad, so very bad. And I still feel bad.

Please write soon,
Ruby Rae

P.S. About this lighting and fabric store queen ... a gay man? Carolyn, really! Talking about something that would drive a girl to drink (hahaha).

February 24

Dear Ruby Rae,

I was deeply touched by your words that spoke of your fearful moment at twilight on the road. Like you, I too chose my mother over my father. Her madness was a shawl that was pockmarked with small areas of loosely woven threads. On those rare days when the sun bled through those sparse patches to soothe Portia with warmth and light, she became a whole and special person, like on the day she rode Grace's new unicycle.

She bought it for Grace with the hope that by riding it, Grace's coordination would improve. While we all stood around the gift, wondering what in the world Grace (or, for that matter, any of us) would do with a unicycle, Hunter chided Portia for buying an inappropriate present. Portia, who spent perhaps fifteen hours a year outdoors (with the bulk of this time spent at garden parties), grabbed the unicycle, sat on it, and rode it down our drive.

We assumed her trip would stop at our driveway's open gates, but she headed down the middle of Sant' Andrea Place and then turned onto Bellagio Road. That's when a bus packed with tourists came down the street to view the homes of the "rich and famous." Unlike us, the tourists had the presence of mind to steady their cameras first on Portia, then on a horrified Hunter, and then on the rest of us as we ran screaming after our Gucci-accessorized mother with pleas to be careful, with pleas to stop. (Or rather, Kip and I ran. Grace remained in the driveway, overcome with giggles.)

We, and the tourists, carried away the memory of having seen a spark of life that day. It was this rarely seen but unforgettable spark that drew me toward Portia, and away from Hunter. I knew Portia was a lot of things, but unlike Hunter, she was never a quitter. Although she had lost her ability to stand up to her brothers and stop their abusive behavior, she nevertheless remained, in some peculiar way, a fighter. She never would allow her challenged child to be warehoused in an institution. (Nor did she ever pretend that Grace wasn't the limited person she is, as Hunter so often did.)

For an adult who wouldn't warehouse her challenged child, it's unfortunate that Portia chose to warehouse her rape by her twin brother, and the feelings — including the rage — from this act of violence. To the outside world, which included her rapist, Portia was, above all else, a lady. A lady's rage must be turned inward if she is to maintain her friendships. A lady must, at all times, be pleasing to society. In Portia's world, a raped woman was something less than pleasing, so a raped woman could not be a lady. As for an incestuous rape — well, in Portia's perfect world, such horrors could not exist. Therefore, I suspect that on some level in her mind, the rape never happened. Ultimately, of course, it was Portia's choice to be a lady. And ultimately, it was the lady in Portia that destroyed her, and nearly destroyed her children.

It was easier for me to forgive Portia for what she did, and didn't do, than it was to forgive Hunter. In part, this is because Portia and I shared the experience of rape. (Although our outcomes from the similar experience were different.) This doesn't make what she did, and didn't do, for her children all right. But it made it easier for me to understand why she chose the path she took. From understanding comes forgiveness.

As for Hunter — well, Hunter was a completely different story. He was harder to understand, and therefore harder to forgive. I'll never forget this one weekend when the infants, Grace and Kip, were at Hunter's parents'. Hunter came home in the wee hours of Sunday morning after spending the bulk of Saturday day, and just about all of its night, with his mistress. During his absence, Portia fell asleep without unlocking the door to my bedroom closet, and releasing me from its darkness.

Portia had imprisoned me shortly before lunch, when she came downstairs and found me making a peanut-butter-

and-honey sandwich. I accidentally dribbled honey on the kitchen counter. The mess caused her to become completely unglued. (Speed freaks flip out over the strangest things. And, when a speed freak is also a womanizer's wife, the combination can result in some frightening fireworks.)

When I heard Hunter come in and walk upstairs, I banged on my closet door. I screamed, "Let me out." Through the closet's locked door, Hunter barked, "Where's the key?" As if I knew. I told him to ask Portia.

He returned with the key, unlocked the door, and shook me by my shoulders. For a full three minutes he yelled at me for being so stupid as to lock myself in the closet. Then and there, at the tender age of six and a half, I had my first inkling that the men in my life would prove themselves to be utterly useless, if not completely lacking in merit. (To survive in a childhood home such as mine, it was necessary to get a grasp on such things as these as early on as possible in life.)

It's difficult to understand and forgive gross stupidity in an otherwise intelligent man. To have to also understand, and then forgive, this man for being utterly useless and without merit is especially difficult when this man is your father. However, I know it can be done, because I have done it. But I wouldn't have been able to do it without my sense of humor.

Carolyn

P.S. What's happening with my short story? If it's too bad to even be talked about, just send it back torn in half.

February 29

Dear Carolyn,

Happy Leap Year, doll ... your favorite holiday, no doubt. Before I forget, I did read your short story and passed it on to my agent. I guess in all that's been going on, or coming up in therapy, I've forgotten all about writing, mine included, so don't take it personally.

I want to start by thanking you for loving me so much. You have been such a great source of love and comfort during these past few trying days. I'm so angry and hurt that I got drunk. Again. How many times will I have to get drunk before I realize that I have a problem with alcohol? I was doing so well, too. I just don't know...

I know this whole incident must seem strange to you. I mean, true, the gas gauge does work on the Mercedes, and I did drive by several gas stations with the warning light on, but the stations were all self-serve ... I'm sorry, Carolyn, but like you just can't eat skins, I just can't pump gas. It's something about the smell.

To make a long story short, I ran out of gas in front of a self-serve gas station. I tried to pay the station attendant to come out and pump it for me. He just said, "Excuse me?" So I went across the street to Maxine's Man Trap Inn, because it looked like the kind of place where men were men and grateful women could get their gas pumped. The next thing I knew, somebody had called Kip to come get me and pay the rest of my bar tab.

Thanks for coming to my defense. God knows I was too hung over to stand up for myself.

Take care...
Ruby Rae

March 6

Dear Ruby Rae,

Odd isn't it, that the fumes from gasoline would drive you to drink an entire fifth and a half of Mr. Daniels? Or was it Jimmy Beam? Oh, Lord! You didn't stoop so low as to pass the time with Old Grandad?

Of course, it has been weeks since your last drink. Perhaps you were making up for lost time? Or, better yet, celebrating a newfound reason to imbibe! Maybe it's time for you to go to an Alcoholics Anonymous meeting. You'll find a listing for the organization in the beginning of your phone directory.

If you ask me (and, yes, I know you haven't. But when has that knowledge ever quieted me?), I suspect the smell of gasoline is a missing piece to the puzzle of your parents' insanity that's stamped on your soul. As the children of Catfyshe and Willie, and Portia and Hunter, crazy-making feelings will forever be at our sides. For me, Portia's incest-loving brothers were all fair-haired and built like wrestlers (albeit, short wrestlers. If they came into this world as dogs, they would definitely be pit bulls). And after having had a blond-haired man with a chest as wide as a refrigerator repeatedly rape me over a period of years, I became programmed to be distrustful of the physical strength behind any muscle-bound man. (Although, I still find them divine to look at.) And no one, including Mr. Beam, will ever be so kind as to shovel this inherited shit for me.

As I once did, you too need to come to define and accept your inheritance. Only then will you be able to befriend your craziness and channel it in creative ways, so you don't die an alcoholic. I think you need to put this binge behind you. Today's a new day, which begs to be lived an hour at a time.

As for the fabric I bought, Molly and I have been having the "bestest" time making drapes and slipcovers. For her upcoming birthday, I may give her a grand piano for her darling Cape Cod dollhouse.

Carolyn

P.S. Speaking of drapes and slipcovers, I keep thinking about Bruce, at Queen Anne's Lighting & Lace, Ltd. He was so adorable, and kind. I want to bake bread with him, but before I do I have to smother my hunger for playful male companionship. I don't want him to think I'm one of those fag hags, who derive crumbs of emotional fulfillment from the gay men in their lives.

Should I bring Rick with me when I go back? His presence will guarantee that my silly emotional needs don't bleed across that store! I don't know why my head's turning this simple bread-baking trip into such a big deal! I mean, Bruce seems happily married to Shawn. And, while I've had my flings, I never fling with happily married. Besides, what well-adjusted queen would even glance at me?

March 13

Dear Carolyn,

This card of the Minnesota state bird (the common loon) reminds me of you. How dare you suggest I attend an AA meeting just because I got a little tipsy over the frustration of having to pump my own gas. I deserved a little drink. It's not like I'm on skid row in a gutter clutching a bottle of Thunderbird. AA, indeed! Why don't you try Man-Anonymous?

Off to Winnifred,
Ruby Rae

March 17

Dearest Ruby Rae,

Normally, one would be offended when told a photograph of the common loon brings oneself to mind. But I know you're in intensive therapy, so I'll just forgive the insult. (Oh, by the way, have I ever mentioned that whenever I see a photo of an ostrich I think of you?)

Anyway, I finally screwed up the courage to phone Bruce about baking bread. When his partner answered my call, Bruce barked "Who? Who?" in the background when Shawn, with great patience, explained I was on the phone. I was crushed. A part of me wanted to slam down the receiver. But I couldn't. My promise wouldn't let me go.

I crossed the shop's threshold with Rick and a sack of flour. All my hatches that covered any need or emotion were firmly sealed. I was coming to make good on my promise, then I was marching from Bruce's life. I wouldn't let him touch me with his playfulness, or kindness, or any of his other "nesses." I'd hide my personality and all its needy defects. I did a fine job until Shawn left to work in his art studio. That's when Bruce took a customer's phone call, and my hungry eyes galloped off to crawl all over him. He just stood at the phone watching me watch him.

He returned to the shop's kitchen, and (I think) he went out of his way to brush his hand against mine as he passed a wooden spoon. I fortunately knew the answer to his test. As long as my eyes stayed glued to the floor, and didn't bounce back into his at the end of the touch, he'd not have a clear view of the silliness in my head: he'd not know I was having an in-lust experience with him.

Ruby Rae, what's wrong with me? The one and only time in my life that I come up against a man who could offer me nothing more than friendship, I completely blow it with my inappropriate needs and lusting. Oh, well, another day of reality at its worst. Let's just hope I get some decent responses to my relationship ad, so I can clear my head of this gay man.

Happy Saint Paddy Day! (Didn't you tell me he's your patron saint?)

Love,
Carolyn

P.S. I just realized, I've never had a male friend who wasn't also my lover.

P.P.S. I can't believe I'm making this a P.P.S.!!! Rick went on a buying craze in the fabric store. Drapes! He ordered drapes for every room in our house (including the bathroom without a window! I told him we have to talk about that!). When he got home, he was on the phone for an hour with Bruce about window measurements. I never knew he had a thing for drapes! Or lighting! You read it right, lighting! Before he left this morning, he told me (and, I mean, told me!) he was going to buy all new lighting for our house. Rick doesn't even like to pick out a color of paint. Sometimes men just do the strangest things. First drapes! And now, lighting! Well, I'll tell you one thing, he's not bringing any crystal chandeliers into this house!

March 27

Dear Carolyn,

I'm too depressed to write, although I don't really know why. It's not your sad, sad, letter about this homosexual, although that is depressing. I think it's maybe because Winnifred and I were talking. I was boasting to her about my oral sexual expertise. (The fact that I can "suck a cantaloupe through the eye of a sewing needle.") She asked me, point-blank, "How'd you learn to give such fabulous head?" I couldn't remember. It certainly wasn't from a lot of experiences. It was like I just always knew. But the thought of it depressed me. Not the thought of giving good head, but the thought of having always known. There I go, smelling that oil and gasoline again. I've been smelling this off and on all afternoon.

Ruby Rae

March 31

Dear Ruby Rae,

How well I remember those months composed of light and dark edges that ran together to haunt me with memories that didn't fit together. The smell of oil and gasoline — I bet, if you're willing to swim through this memory's pain to reach the shore of its other side, you'll find a story or two to enrich your work.

Time is a gift. Use it. When you're ready, your horror scraps will too magically slip together.

I love you,
Carolyn

April 6

Dear Carolyn,

Thanks for the warm note. But when I want your advice I'll ask for it. Since when did you hang out a shingle, other than maybe "Justice of the Peace ... bride included"? There are no memories to wade through as far as the smells of oil and gasoline are concerned. I didn't want to have to tell you this, but for your information I have a very rare, undetectable-by-scan brain tumor. Nothing is more obnoxious than a dime-store side-street shrink. Oh by the way, I'm in *People* magazine this week.

Sincerely,
Ruby Rae

P.S. Don't you just love the picture of the chickadee (the state bird of Massachusetts) on the front of this postcard?

April 13

Ruby Rae,

I guess your last message was sent to prove that prolonged sobriety and abstinence suit you about as well as horizontal stripes. Besides, do you honestly expect me to be impressed by some blurred picture of you that appears on the very, very back page of a magazine I'd only buy if it came pre-wrapped in brown paper? (I mean, *Playgirl* is one thing, but *People?* Darling, I do have some standards!)

Carolyn

P.S. What is with you and these postcards of state birds? Perhaps, you should consider discussing this new fixation with Winnifred.

P.P.S. And speaking of Winnifred, I had your same tumor years ago. Only, my "tumor" wasn't in my brain.

P.P.P.S. I just got a phone call from Molly's mother. She sounded really upset. We're having lunch next week.

April 14

Dear Diary,

First I have a tumor. Then I don't. Then I do. Then I don't. Now I'm mad. Then I'm not mad. I'm a drunk. Fine. I'll be all of these things and more.

But just one thing ... cut off my ribs, cut off my booze, cut off my tumor, but leave that one-eyed, purple-veined, moisture-seeking, ballistic wand of rapture, doom, and bliss alone! I have got to have something to live for; not to mention something to die for.

Read 'em and weep ... Kip hasn't slam-dunked me into the cheap seats in weeks. I'm so horny I called up the operator and asked for the area code for Nome, Alaska. I was gonna call up a man and talk dirty. I figured my odds of finding a lonely man was much higher in Nome. What did I get? St. Jerome's Rectory, in downtown Nome. Kip will pay for this.

I think he must be having an affair. Somebody called here last week and when I answered the phone they said, "Oh, I must have the wrong number." It's the oldest trick in the book. Catfyshe may have had her problems but there were some things she knew about ... namely, men. And I remember Mamma used to say, "If you're sitting up there in heat, it's because your old man hasn't turned your damper down, and that's because he's been busy using his tools on some other furnace across town."

I give up. I'm going to take my friend Shelly's advice and do what she does when she's horny. I'm going shopping!

Ruby

April 20

Dear Ruby Rae,

I've just suffered through one of the most dreadful afternoons in my adult life. I met Molly's mother, Meg, at that trendy bistro in Whitefish Beach. She was twenty minutes late. She said her meeting with her clients had "run over." (From the way she looked, one would think that she had just been run over. Yes, I know this sounds like a comment that came from your mouth. Right now, I feel as if my whole entire life came from your mouth on a morning after a night you partied with Jim Beam.)

Anyway, you were right about what I was doing to Molly. At least, I think you were right. Right now, I feel so detached from my life and myself, that you could tell me my last name was Punaro, and I'd agree with you.

Meg got down to the chase scene as soon as we took up our respective salad forks and started spearing green things. Anyhow, the long and the short of it is, she wants me to be "less available to Molly." While I've been "well intentioned" my "overindulgence of her child" has "undermined the limits" that Meg has been trying to impose on her daughter. How was I to know Molly was having behavioral problems at school, if no one told me? (Or at least told me in English.)

Anyway, I assured Meg that I wasn't trying to do anything that would further Molly's little problems. I was just trying to love a child who's unhappy because she always comes home to a Slavic-speaking housekeeper. And I certainly didn't know she'd stolen all that dollhouse furniture from that girl in her class! As I said to Meg, had I known this I wouldn't have sat up all those nights making custom slipcovers for it!

As you implied months ago, I wanted a child to love me so I could feel that had I been able to have children, I would have been a special parent. Well, it was this and the fact that I need someone with whom to celebrate life. A child makes a good companion for celebrating being alive.

In light of all of this, it's not surprising I let Molly walk all over me.

After lunch, I sat down at my computer (tonight's my first meeting with my writers' group), and I went over my novel's first three chapters. I know the work is good, and I feel proud to share it with other writers. Once the pages were printed, I stood in my quiet house. As the minutes passed, the quiet seemed to fold in on itself, and with each silent fold, the house seemed to be a vast echo of emptiness rather than a home.

I went downstairs, and phoned a couple of people, who are good acquaintances, but not deep-in-my-gut friends. Our conversations only made the silence in my house feel worse. I couldn't spend another moment in the house, so I got in my car and drove past the lighting and fabric store. But I felt lonely — too lonely — to dare go in. I drove around town for an hour while I waited for my workshop to begin.

Carolyn

April 21

Dear Ruby Rae,

It's three in the morning. (Rick has been at the hospital since one.) I know, I just wrote you about twelve hours ago. But the pit of my stomach is racing like the Bullet Train. I can't think straight. I'm just too damned tangled up in feelings. The wrong feelings. The scary feelings. The feelings that drive you to phone one of those suicide hot lines. I'm alone. I'm utterly and completely alone. I have to get out of here.

I'm back. You won't believe what I did. I drove to the lighting and fabric store and peered (for only god knows how long) through its well-lighted window. I'd still be there if that police car hadn't pulled up, and Officer Clinton hadn't asked what I was up to. I lied and said I was looking for my husband. Technically, it wasn't a lie. I've spent the last eighteen years looking for my husband. Of course, his name and face always change, but still, it's always the same husband.

My abortion and sterilization have driven me too close to the edge. The edge that's no wider than a single, black thread. If I don't get a grip on myself, I'll soon find myself walking it like it's a tightrope. A thread is not a rope of hope above a black abyss. A thread is just a thread. Once I walk on it, its fibers will break, and I will fall into my madness. To die of madness is, I believe, the worst of all slow deaths, because of the vulnerability of its victims. If I am to be mad, then I shall maintain my dignity by giving myself a very quick death.

That liquid morphine left over from Hunter — Rick thought I poured out the last bottle. It was full — well — almost full. (Hunter only used a few tablespoons of the half-quart.) I can't find it. The almost-full half-quart. I can't find it. I hid it for a night like this, so I could waltz with death. Do you have it? — Hunter's morphine? Do you have it, Ruby Rae? Did you take it? It's mine, Ruby Rae. It's mine.

If only someone had answered my relationship ad. I'm not even worth the price of a first-class stamp. Life would be so much easier if I were dead.

Carolyn

VIA FEDERAL EXPRESS

April 21

Ruby Rae!

Look, I just sent you a letter that wasn't meant for you! It was postmarked the 21st. Don't open it! Just send it right back. Okay? If you do this, I swear, I'll never ever bring up what you did at Christmas. I promise. Never! Just send back the letter unopened.

Thanks!
Carolyn

P.S. Next to Grace, you're the best sister I ever had!

April 25

Dear Carolyn,

I'm returning your letter. I assume it's a letter to one of these ad people ... or some other man. But "judge not lest ye be judged..."

I know you won't believe this, but I'm sorry about you and Molly. If there's anything I know about, it's emptiness. Emptiness in houses that seem to go on forever.

I've started remembering more things, before nine. I can relate to relying on a crumb of attention or kindness from neighbors in order to survive, so I can understand what it must be like for Molly to come home to a housekeeper who she can't communicate with. And I feel for you ... the boogeymen are even scarier for big girls trapped in empty houses.

Let me tell you what Christmas was like for me when I was between the ages of four and eight. I would wake up to an empty house, except for the rats and me, and a few toys scattered under the Christmas tree. I would run to the window, and confirm my worst fear. They were gone; I would see my parents' footprints leading off in opposite directions in the snow, each of them gone to the refuge of their lovers' arms.

I'd start crying, eating, and wondering if they were going to come back and when. Then I'd look and see how much coal there was and start gathering Grandma's old quilts and laying them by the old Round Oak stove so they'd be nice and warm in case I ran out of coal. The winters in Michigan could be lethal in an uninsulated tar paper shack with no fire, especially if my parents were gone for a day or two.

Then I'd clean up the mess from the fight. There was always a fight. And just like there was always a fight, there was always a mess. I remember one year Mamma broke an entire set of dishes except the gravy bowl. The only reason she didn't break that was because she was drinking her vodka and Kool-Aid out of it. I remember the dining room had broken dishes an inch deep all over the floor.

After that I'd take my teddy bear, a gift that got me through Christmas when I was five, cuddle up under the blankets, and go to sleep watching TV. Some Christmases (the good ones), when I'd wake up Daddy would be back home and passed out drunk underneath the Christmas tree, clutching a holiday twelve-pack of Budweiser, with the imprint of the raised Budweiser holiday logo embedded in the side of his face. Then Mamma would appear ... Or, was this dastardly apparition an angel from Christmas hell? Her head looked like her neck had thrown up and somebody had tossed her face on it with a pitchfork. Mamma's hair pointed toward every major city in the Western Hemisphere, and her eyes looked like two meatballs on a plate of spaghetti. Yes, it was the familiar holiday stench of wanton whiskey sluts and sweaty steelworkers, and not holly, that filled the air at Christmas.

Love ya,
Ruby Rae

P.S. Hope your writers' group went okay. If it didn't, go shopping. My girlfriend Shelly is right. If done right, shopping can be orgasmic. Gotta go try on clothes!

April 29

Dear Ruby Rae,

Thanks for sending my letter back unopened. Going to the writers' group was a fun kind of scary experience. It was great connecting up with other writers — two of the group members are in the process of having their first books published — but it was scary reading my work aloud knowing that once I was through, I'd hear these stranger's comments. Most were encouraging, and the ones that weren't were still very helpful. Finally I've met people who have things in common with me. If only I could meet a man who shares my same interests. (As luck would have it, the only two men in the writers' group are married.)

As for my Christmas memories, the fabulousness of the day lay in the fact it was the nearest taste our family ever had of normalcy. Portia was so civil to Hunter and us kids, you could almost pretend she was some Donna Reed who didn't live her life with the help of pills. And, in honor of the holiday, our uncles' lust for us never amounted to anything more than a few sick looks and inappropriate touches.

But for you, the day was like any other day, the craziness was out of its box. For you, there wasn't twenty-four hours of peace on earth. I think that twenty-four-hour reprieve did much to maintain my sanity. It was a moment of calm to look forward to, and then, once it passed, it was a moment to which I could cling when Portia locked me in a closet and left for the day, or her brother yet again raped me. You know, Ruby Rae, the only good that comes from our childhood memories is that they allow us, as adults, to reconnect with our parents' insanity, to show us we weren't in any way responsible for the dysfunctional households of our youths.

And speaking of dysfunctional, your thoughts seemed a bit scattered in your last letter. I'm a bit concerned about your latest interest in shopping. Do you still see Winnifred? You haven't spoken of her lately.

As for what's happening with me, I miss Molly a lot. We wave to each other, and sometimes talk over the fence, but the connection we once had is no longer there. I just ache for someone to love who will love me back. If only Bruce wasn't gay, then I bet you anything the needs I have would be met in this life.

Oh, and speaking of needs, I do have some good news: the newspaper that ran my relationship ad phoned. My reply box is absolutely overflowing! Each time I think of getting in my car to drive to the City, I feel so lonely, so embarrassed, and — I don't know, desperate — that I just can't bring myself to make the trip. But I'll find my nerve the next time I'm feeling lonely.

Loving you,
Carolyn

P.S. If you think shopping can be orgasmic, try opening a few issues of *Playgirl!* At least that's what I do when I get "the urge." (Well, it's either that, or I have my sinfully private visions of that too, too gorgeous, and as I like to dream, sensual, Bruce.) — Too bad you're too righteous to be that sinful on your own. I bet with Kip you're willing to do all sorts of naughty French things. (Not to mention that little trick you perform with a cantaloupe.)

As a present for Kip (who I know hates large, outstanding bills), I'm shipping you my back issues of *Playgirl*. You can tuck them under all those back issues of *Bride* magazine that Kip told me he found tucked in your hope chest last week.

P.P.S. By the way, any word from your agent about my short story?

May 3

Dear Carolyn,

This will probably be the last letter I write to anybody. Why? Because if Kip doesn't kill me, some prison gang will. I added up my shopping spree bills today. I can't believe this. I spent $31,856.87 on that shopping trip I took with that goddamned, big-thighed, bagel-biting, diet-soda-slurping, label-addict, whiny, refuse-to-pay-for-parking Shelly. I'm not speaking to that Hebraic bitch. I can't believe this. I knew I spent a lot, maybe five grand, but thirty-one? I guess I wasn't really adding it up in my head.

How can I tell Kip that I charged fifteen thousand dollars' worth of clothes and accessories on his credit cards and wrote another fifteen thousand dollars' worth of bad checks on our joint account? And the only thing I can take back is one pair of unopened panty hose that I got in a larger size than usual "just to see," which may be the only thing that truly fits.

And that's not even the worst of it. I just got a royalty check for $639.14, marked "account paid in full for quarter." I can't believe I'm out of royalty checks and won't see another one until the next quarter, which is months away, and my publisher said that I should expect a tiny one, because my book has stopped selling. What am I going to do, Carolyn? I'm in debt $31,856.87, and I don't have an income. Sure, I'm writing another book, but by the time I see money from that I will be well settled into my early grave.

I can't believe I've done this. I'm so disappointed in myself. I really am. I thought I learned this lesson with my first checking account in high school. If not then, I thought for sure I had this lesson down by the time they closed my seventeenth checking account a few months ago at the Worker's Bank of Taipei ... It's a simple rule: don't write checks on money that's not actually in the account ... I just don't understand why I did this. Well, I'm going to have to have an emergency session with Winnifred. That's the good news. The bad news is I'm going to have to write her a check.

In the grips of grief,
Ruby Rae

P.S. What I really need is my father's rabbit gun, so I could just put myself in the ground and be over it.

May 9

Dear Ruby Rae,

Well, now we know why Winnifred hasn't gotten out of those old, sling-back shoes: uncollected funds.

If your letter hadn't saddened me as it did, I'd also quip that a rabbit gun isn't sufficiently large for the intended target. But, quip or not, there's truth in the thought. A gun is not the tool you need. The tool you need is truth. — I'm surprised Winnifred hasn't mentioned that you can only be as sick as your secrets. I don't know what you have tucked inside you, but from your recent behavior, I can say I've stood close to where you stand now, and I was able to survive, so don't be afraid. Life is waiting for you on the other side of the darkness.

Hopefully, your despair and panic have lifted, or at least become numb. When I ride a blue streak, I often remind myself that for a crazy person, I'm relatively sane, and that sane people are in part sane because their healthy psyches won't let them wade through more shit than can be handled at one time. Perhaps my theory is absolute crap, but it's carried me through some bleak times.

As for me, I think I'm working through the problem areas in my novel. The consensus of my writers' workshop seems to be that it's only a few chapters away from being ready to be submitted. Pretty exciting!

Oh, and speaking of exciting, I went and picked up the responses to my relationship ad. Ninety-nine percent of the men are fools and grunions, but the other one percent — well, let's just say they are one hell of a one percent. Now all I need to do is to is send the three finalists a playful little letter and my picture! I think I'll do it tonight while Rick is at one of his many committee meetings.

Take care and God bless,
Carolyn

P.S. Have you heard of Debtors Anonymous? Since you feel vulnerable right now, why not let some insights surface via your feelings? At least consider it, okay?

May 13

Dear Carolyn,

Thank you for your warm letter. It shed some much-needed light. I can't believe this. Kip does love me. He loves me a lot. He's not even that upset about the shopping spree. He just put me on a strict budget ... and I know I'm going to be real good. I feel in control and fabulous again.

I ran into this homosexual who is into sadomasochism at Winnifred's office. We were talking, and I told him I wasn't into pain. He looked down at my spikes and said, "Oh, please, girl ... those shoes."

The man had a point. So I finally talked Kip into beating me with a belt. I loved it. Kip hated it. I don't understand. Why won't he beat me? He says he loves me too much and that he just can't bear to hurt me like that. I say, if he loved me, he'd beat me. He says I should talk to Winnifred. I say, a belt's only twelve bucks and will last for a long time, Winnifred's $100 an hour and there's no guarantee. And even when he did beat me, he didn't beat me hard. Not like Daddy would have. I've got to get him a better belt, one like Daddy's: a big long black one ... belt, I mean.

All kidding aside, I really think I have a brain tumor, Carolyn. I keep getting the salty taste of blood in my mouth but there's no blood there. And I have these flashes of something that I can't quite make out. The flashes last only a second, like a test for the Emergency Broadcast System on TV, then they're gone. Then I smell coal dust, then I smell oil and gasoline, but there is no coal dust, no oil, no gasoline. I don't understand. I'll write more later...

Ruby Rae

May 17

Dear Ruby Rae,

The delicate relationship between your sense of inner peace and self-acceptance, and your need for abuse, stuns me. Tranquility shouldn't come to you when you're black-and-blue, or drunk, or in debt. You might discuss this with Winnifred.

And, speaking of the delicate relationship between inner peace and self-acceptance, mine too is out of balance. It's Molly. I've completely blown it. Last night Meg phoned and told me I could never see her daughter again. The edict hit me from out of the blue. — When we had lunch, Meg only asked me to make myself "less available" to her child and, when I did see her, "to be mindful of the fact that Molly was in need of well-defined limits and bounds." By the end of our lunch, I thought I understood exactly what those limits and bounds are.

When I picked up Molly from school, as Meg had asked me to do (Olga is off for a three-day weekend), we shared hugs and kisses, and a long chat about what had been happening in her life. As we turned onto the highway, she thanked me for the drapes for her dollhouse (we delicately ignored the slipcovers). Then she asked if we could go to the boardwalk and ride the roller coaster. I told her we couldn't, because her mother only allowed those types of outings on special days, and this was not a special day. But when Molly looked up at me with her big, green, smiling eyes and said in a voice that quivered (with joy?) that this was a special day because she hadn't seen me for so long, I didn't think it would be wrong to take her to the tea room in Lofton's Department Store. She looked so adorably impish when she smiled and said, "Lofton's makes just the bestest caramel sundaes."

Granted, I was intent on showing her a good time. And maybe, if I hadn't been, I would have noticed she lingered longer than usual at the store's makeup counter. (When we go to Lofton's we always try on lipstick.) So, when Meg phoned saying that Molly had taken all those sample lipsticks — well, naturally I was shocked.

In hindsight, I guess it was my fault for not properly supervising her. But Meg's tone seemed so unnecessarily accusatory that, well, the next thing I told her was "If you made more effort to make each of Molly's days feel special, your daughter wouldn't have to steal to get her only parent's attention."

Admittedly, my comment was out of line. But don't you agree that Meg was equally out of line to say I'm to never again spend time with her child? Shit! If you could have heard Meg's tone, you'd think that I'd helped Molly steal those six tubes of lipstick.

On top of this, Rick just left for a four-day convention in New Orleans. I asked to go along, but he said I wouldn't have much fun, because he'd be in meetings all day. That's just what you'd expect to hear from a man. They never make themselves available when you really need them. — Even Bruce and Shawn are gone. (They're celebrating their ten-year anniversary with a Tahitian honeymoon.) I guess I wouldn't feel so down if one of the three men who were the finalists from my relationship ad had replied to my letters.

Nobody wants me. I feel so worthless. No matter how well intentioned I might be, nothing ever seems to work for me. My life is one big, long punishment for something I don't remember doing in a previous life, so I know it couldn't have even been much fun.

Oh, well, at least I have one thing that no one can take from me: my writing. It's the only thing from which I get any positive feedback. Well, it's that and my friendship with you. I mean, even when you're drunk, you love me, don't you, Ruby Rae? You do love me, and always will no matter what, won't you?

Wishing you'd come for a long, long visit,
Carolyn

May 18

Dear Diary

Oh, what a day! I still think the reason Kip won't beat me is because he's got a bitch on the side. Like Catfyshe used to say ... "It ain't no good until it hurts a little bit" ... so why won't he beat me? Obviously ... because he's got a bitch on the side. You don't have to be Catfyshe to figure some things out.

Well, I've been trying to catch him in the act. Today I was sure I saw him in his car, and his mistress was in it. I chased the car down, and at a stoplight, I jumped out and snatched the bitch out of the car ... Just when I was about to slap her drawers off, her husband jumped out from the driver's side. That's right ... her husband, not mine. Oh, it was an ugly mess. The police came ... I had to explain ... thank God I'm in therapy ... They called Winnifred and she came and retrieved me from the police station.

We had an emergency session. She claims there is no real evidence of an affair. She claims that I'm becoming an adrenaline junkie ... and what I'm into is the rush of adrenaline I get when I think I'm busting Kip in the act of wrong ... and I pay for this nonsense.

Ruby Rae

May 18

Ruby Rae!

I got a response! A positive response, from my number-one finalist who answered my relationship ad. Morgan! That's his name. Morgan. Just like the horse. (Dare I hope he's hung like his namesake?) He's a bit tied up with work, so we can't meet till July 20th (boo-hoo). I can't wait! But till then, we'll talk on the phone. He has just the sexiest voice. His vowels sound deep, and gnarled, like muscles running down — well, get out your *Playgirls*, and see for yourself.

Off to the gym for my new man!

Carolyn

P.S. By the way, do you know a polite way to ask someone if they are infected with herpes, or are HIV-positive? Things have certainly changed since the time I was between my third and fourth husbands!

May 18

Dear Diary,

I don't know why I ever listen to Carolyn. How dare she get me involved with this big-thighed, bristly haired heifer Winnifred. And what kind of name is that for a bitch anyway ... Winnifred ... sounds like something a bitch with her looks would travel across the country in.

Let me tell you what this wide-bodied buffalo did. Besides this adrenaline nonsense ... she was very "curious" (of course) about this memory I have of Daddy and me taking baths, and of the smells and tastes I've been having from my brain tumor. (Even though my doctor's tests say I don't have a brain tumor, we know I do.)

Anyway, I was mentioning to her again, just in passing, that I was fabulous at giving head. She asked me, again, where did I learn to give such "fabulous" head? And again I couldn't remember. But I knew it wasn't from Kip or my other boyfriend. I just have always known somehow. The thought of this makes me depressed, and I smell oil and gasoline. I'm sure I have a brain tumor. And I need some tumor medicine ... if you know what I mean.

Ruby Rae

May 20

Dear Carolyn,

I've tried to ignore all of your foolishness. As for your wanting to know a tasteful way to ask if somebody is HIV-positive ... that's like trying to figure out a tasteful way to ask for the money when you're done. Please, girl, get a grip. And about this Morgan ... honey ... I don't believe you. You are definitely not shipping a full seed bag.

Furthermore, I suppose you're satisfied now. I had to see Winnifred for an extra session this week, 'cause we've started talking about the baths that I used to take with Daddy when I was little. Winnifred said I grabbed my throat when I started talking about the baths. She asked me if I learned to give good head from Daddy. I almost slapped that heifer's drawers off. (Assuming she was wearing some.) How dare she suggest such a thing! If I wasn't such a classy bitch, I would've broken some artillery out on her ass and blown that tacky dress right off her back. God knows if dressing tacky was a crime, she'd be on death row.

Anyway, I turned over her desk and told her to kiss me where the mailman don't go and walked out. Of all the nerve suggesting something like that! I've got to find a new shrink. On second thought, I'm over shrinks and all of your suggestions!

Livid, livid, livid,
Ruby Rae

May 22

Dear Ruby Rae,

So, you're toying with the prospect of stopping therapy? Trust me, I know all about it. I mean, do you honestly think that you are Winnie's first "client" (why can't they just call us patients when they are so goddamned blunt about everything else?) who has toppled her desk as a means to assert control over the relationship? Darling, please, if you were meant to be the top in the relationship, you wouldn't write "Winnie" a monthly check!

As for toppling her desk, trust me, you aren't the first who has succeeded at that. (Or worse. You know the tank of fish she has? The fish that are meant to be soooo soothing? At your next appointment ask her about the "client" who swallowed her two favorite fish, Jung and Kierkegaard, because she wouldn't stop talking incest. Next to that your little scene with the desk will seem like nothing, and the air will be cleared.)

As for smells, you're also not her first "client" to smell things associated with their rape. For me, it was popcorn. (Which explains why for years I couldn't go to the movies.) Nor will your memories' stench fade if you stop therapy. Oil-and-gasoline-type memories are complex, and peculiar in their dormant makeup. Once they pop forth, their force is such that they often can't be "restuffed."

I think your life will be much harder and scarier if you stop your sessions with Winnifred. Like all survivors of child abuse, you'd rather keep your past hidden. Trust me. Like you, I once tried to run. By the time I wised up and returned to Winnifred, I was in a far worse place than you now are. I'd hate to see you tumble into that hell.

You can trust Winnifred. She knows what she's doing. Write soon. I want to know how you are.

A very, very concerned,
Carolyn

May 23

Ruby Rae!

Not only am I still concerned about you, I'm concerned about myself! The woman who ran Queen Anne's Lighting & Lace, Ltd., while Bruce and Shawn were away told me that they would be back last weekend. So, today, I dropped by to see them. I really didn't need to buy material to re-upholster our family room couch. But, I didn't think Bruce would want to see me unless I came as a customer.

When I walked through his shop's door, he said a pleasant "hello" and asked after Rick and our new drapes. He said Rick hadn't gotten back to him about getting new lighting, and he looked forward to hearing from him. Then he offered me a generous discount on certain bolts of fabric that would match our new window treatments. As I studied material and spoke with him, I realized I'd do just about anything to be a cat who could nap on his lap while he loved and petted me. Soon thereafter, I was touched by a sadness that begged to spend an entire night with him, laughing and talking and baking oatmeal cookies while becoming friends.

I drove home in circles. Each wrong turn found me thinking, So what if I yearn for the focused attention that would come from Bruce, if he drew me into an intense, caring friendship? This need in me isn't a biggie! And even if it is, I don't care to deal with it now. For were I to look at my need under the light of reality, I'd have to deal with the sad fact that Bruce and I are never going to spend a night baking cookies, or spend any part of any night doing anything together. At times like this, I wish my mental health was in bad enough straits that I could cling to some happy delusions. But I'll never have the luck to be in such straits, any more than I'll be in the lucky position of being accepted as a friend by Shawn and his mate. Life is full of disappointments, and this is just one of them.

I know that a 35-year-old woman with a crush on a queen just isn't a pretty sight. But this isn't really a crush or romance thing. It's a feeling-lonely thing. It's a cry for companionship. That's all it is. What's going down here is sure to pass. I'm just stuck in a weird place. I really, really, really love Rick! If I didn't, I wouldn't have stayed five years.

Maybe I'm too burned-out from unrequited love to acknowledge what I need from Rick, and then demand that he make an effort to meet these needs. I think deep down I haven't done this because if things didn't change after my demand, I'd have to move on. Again. The humiliation of yet another failure!

Why I'm going through this when I have Morgan waiting in the wings for a fling? Well, sort of waiting. I haven't spoken to him in a couple of days. Shit! Isn't a career supposed to be the solution to my problem? I have a career. I write every day. So, why do I always come back to this same place in all my relationships? Why am I doing whatever it is that I am doing wrong? It is wrong. It's all god-awful wrong.

Send any and all answers that you might have to help me.

Love,
A very troubled Carolyn

P.S. Maybe, life will seem less bleak once my novel and short story sell.

May 27

Dear Diary,

Why didn't the Mother Church canonize Jack Daniels, the patron saint of tumors? I think he's a saint. I feel much better now.

I've invented a new drink ... the Ruby Rae Tumor Buster. Three shots of Jack Daniels and a shot of morphine. Yes, somehow that liquid morphine left over from Hunter got in my purse today ... and it's a lovely shade of blue.

Speaking of blue ... dear Carolyn is so blue ... and I've forgiven her now for getting me involved with Winnifred. So I've decided to cheer her up. I just happen to have a little stationery from my agent. I'm going to write her a nice little encouraging note from Bernie. That'll cheer her up...

Love and kissie wissies...
Ruby Rae
a.k.a. Bernie Goldstein ...
agent to the stars

UNITED WRITERS' AGENCY
From the Desk of
BERNARD GOLDSTEIN

May 27

Dear Ms. Spencer,

Thank you for submitting your short story, "The Pond in the Silver Winter." Not only did I enjoy it, I passed it on to the *New Yorker.* You are a very talented writer, with a very bright future. I look forward to the opportunity of representing you.

I will be out of town for a few weeks. I will call you when I return.

Keep writing,
Bernie Goldstein

BG/rf

June 3

Dear Ruby Rae,

I'm as happy as a bug in June! You're the "bestest" thing that ever happened in my life. Bernie loves my work! My workshop loves my work! And if things keep going like this, the *New Yorker* will love my work! It looks like your good buddy Bernie is going to get my short story published! And when it happens, I'm driving down to L.A. and treating Bernie and you to lunch at Spago's. He's such a fabulous agent! He wrote me a letter on Memorial Day?! To do that, he must really love my work!!!!!

Oodles and oodles of love,
Carolyn

June 8

Carolyn,

Congratulations on your success with Bernie. I had a feeling he would like your work. But in a more serious vein, as long as we're confronting what's really going on and being genuinely concerned ... Why don't you put some of the energy you put into toying with this fabric/lighting store queen into your relationship with Rick. Huh? Why don't you take your loneliness and grab it by the horns and face it straight on? Are you afraid you'll end up locked in the closet all day long again? Case in point: you didn't even mention sharing your success with Rick.

Come out of the closet, Carolyn, and speak up and be heard. It's all right. Nobody's going to hurt you for being human and having human needs this time. You're in my prayers. I've gotta go. Don't ask me why, but I've decided to take your advice and go see Winnifred again, even though I'm positive I am not a victim of incest.

Love ya,
Ruby Rae

June 11

Shit, Ruby Rae!

"Why don't you take your loneliness and grab it by the horns and face it straight on?" Hell! I'd love to discuss my loneliness or my writing successes with Rick. But each time I try, he's either paged by the hospital to perform an emergency operation, or he says that as a surgeon, time is too much of a luxury for him to waste it on indulging in navel gazing or feeling feelings.

Why can't our marriage be more than two people just sharing a bed? Why can't we also laugh, and play, and hold each other through the night, and go to movies, for walks on the beach, and out to dinner, and talk about things? Why do we work, work, work, and then take five minutes for some unsatisfying sex once every eight weeks? Because Rick is a surgeon, who wears a beeper twenty-four hours a day, seven days a week, that's why. As he often reminds me (verbally and otherwise), on the day we met he made it quite clear his patients would always come first. Oh, well, the good news is Rick's not a liar!

I guess I either didn't understand what Rick meant, or thought his priorities would change. Shit! I've done it again. I've gotten into another relationship where I thought someone would love me enough to change their ways. Not very educable, am I? Oh, well, as somebody famous once said, "Mistakes only become errors when we don't admit to them."

As for Bruce, I'm still stuck on him. For me to keep him as my lust-object even though he lacks chest hairs (and weeks upon weeks of bedroom fantasies that can't get underway until I redecorate his upper torso by moving Shawn's luscious salt-and-pepper chest hairs onto him) just further suggests the extent to which feelings of beyond-lust are going down with me. The experience has proved to be worse than a very bad case of the clap! All I can say is, it's my eighth-grade crush on Tommy Andrews all over again. Only this time out, Tommy's not in love with Rita — he's gay! And I can fantasize about

Bruce till I'm blue in the face from multiple orgasms, but you and I know my most impressive redecorating feat doesn't lie in moving around some chest hairs: it lies in picturing a gay man as straight! Damn Rick! If he wanted me for his lover, I'd not feel so damned randy when I think of Bruce!

I'd not mind so much that Rick doesn't want me as a lover if he'd show me, in some small way, that I'm important to him. So many hours of my day are spent doing things that make his life easier: personal errands, the overspill work from his office, all our banking and investing, all our tax and pension plan filings, not to mention writing his family and picking up after him! Is it too much to ask (or expect) him to spend a few minutes each day focused on me and my needs? I'm tired of asking him if he thinks I'm pretty, or if he loves me, or if I make him happy. Don't tell me. I know. I'm so busy taking care of him that I don't let him know my needs. Long ago, I had this intellectual breakthrough. I'm still waiting for the corresponding emotional breakthrough.

And speaking of waiting, Morgan still hasn't returned my phone call to him last week. He's probably married. I guess I'll have to take out a new relationship ad, since I haven't heard a thing from my two runners-up. I know this will sound like I have a real bad case of the "pitiful pearl pathetics," but a part of me had hoped Rick would see my relationship ad, and would answer it.

I wonder what Bruce would say if I went to his shop and just asked him to pretend to love me for a day? Now I am sounding desperate and lacking in any and all pride. But the way I feel now, a loss of pride is a small expenditure to pay for a day of being held, for a day of make-believe love. I'd better get my dog, Petunia, and take her for a walk. I need to clear my head.

I hope life for you has calmed. It pleases me that you've remained with Winnifred.

Carolyn

P.S. Incest victim!? Please! Try, incest survivor!

June 12

Dear Carolyn,

I can't remember a sadder time in my life than right now. I've been lying here crying all day long. You're not going to believe what I have to tell you. Here's how it happened: I was in the shower and it just flashed out in my mind, like one of those tests for the Emergency Broadcast System interrupting a rerun: Daddy crawling on top of me. I can't believe this. This is just too terrible to be true. I knew my father had his faults, but not this. This is just too perverse. I want to tell my mamma, but she ain't here, just like she wasn't there when it happened. Only this time she ain't never coming back. I want to tell my sister and my brother, but I just know that they would never believe me.

In many ways, Daddy was the hero. He worked in that awful steel mill so that we would have food and clothes. Nobody would believe me. They would think it's just my imagination. And they might be right. I may very well have lost my mind. After all, why didn't I remember this earlier? Why can't I remember exact dates and times? And why can't I remember the whole thing? Why, why, why? I need wine. No, I don't need wine. I need a friend ... I need my best friend ... Master Jack D...

Ruby Rae

June 17

Dear Ruby Rae,

When I was with Winnifred, she taught me it's common for incest survivors to have memory blocks. The gaps are survival tools that have the potential to become daggers if the "forgotten" issues aren't addressed at some later point in life.

When I told Hunter about my experiences with Portia's brother, he replied I had to learn the "ins and outs" of sex from someone, so I might as well lay back and enjoy it. He wasn't in the least concerned, or sensitive to the fact, that at age twelve my biggest secret was my monthly fear that my period was late because I was pregnant. After Portia died, he added that he didn't see my rapes as "big deals" since Portia had been raped by her twin brother and she survived it.

On the night Portia died, Kip and Grace admitted that for years Portia's three brothers had raped them. I insisted they not be at her funeral. But Hunter was too full of boo-hoos to be a man. He broke down and let all the brothers come and sit beside us in the family pew.

A week after the funeral, Hunter invited the pedophiles to dinner. He wanted them to feel he and his raped children felt no ill will toward them. He also wanted to send Grace and Kip to a shrink (selected by the pedophiles), who would determine if they had spoken truthfully about the rapes. I would have none of his ideas, and found a lawyer. But, at that time in the state of California the right to prosecute your childhood molester was forfeited twelve months after your twenty-first birthday. Since then, the state's legislature and governor have passed a law that extends the statute of limitations in abuse cases to the age of twenty-six and, in certain cases, allows victims at whatever age to bring action up to three years after their discovery of their childhood injury, if there is a connection between their present psychological, physical, or emotional problems and their sexual molestation. Similar laws are in effect in Alaska, Colorado, Maine, Montana, and Washington. But for those states that have not followed suit, one must ask if the governors and legislatures of these states have such small brains they can't comprehend that the power a molester wields over a child doesn't instantly vanish when a child turns twenty-one? (On the surface it appears the answer is yes, their brains are small. But perhaps more honestly, their brains are the same size as their constituents, since they seem to agree that there isn't a need for such laws to be passed.)

I found it hard to forgive Hunter for the way he handled the mess, until I realized I couldn't expect anything more from a man who repeatedly allowed Portia's brothers to physically beat him in front of his children, never stood up to his wife when she abused her children, and laughed when I told him the police had come to the house, again. Somewhere along the way, Hunter lost sight of the man he could be, and of his potential for greatness. Perhaps this explains why he and Portia hooked up and stayed together. They were bullies who became allies through their direct and indirect abuse of their children, which they mistook as a salve for the childhood wounds that united them.

I sometimes wonder if Portia and Hunter would have married if Portia hadn't been raped. She was so concerned with maintaining a "good appearance" that she was probably painfully aware that in the 1940s a nonvirgin woman might have "less value" to a marriage-minded man. Hunter, in his very unpredictable "liberal way," probably didn't give a damn about her virginity. Of course, his liberal ways also blocked out the need to get Portia and their children as far away as they could from her family. There is forgiveness, and then there is blind forgiveness. Blind forgiveness too often exacts too high a toll.

I've shared this with you not to put your pain after mine, but to tell you you're not alone in your experience. The pain can be survived without the aid of bourbon. I know you think the pain will kill you. But it won't. I've been there, and I came back in one piece, without taking a single drink.

As for your siblings believing your incest experiences — well, well, well. You might discover the hell didn't happen only to you.

I wish more than anything that I could give you a hug right now,

Carolyn

P.S. Now, for the good news. Shawn is moving to Italy! (He's accepted a tenured university position teaching classical painting.) Naturally, Bruce can't stand in Shawn's career pathway, any more than he can bring himself to sell Queen Anne's Lighting & Lace, Ltd. So, he's leasing out Shawn's art studio and helping him pack (through tears). They say they plan to holiday together at least twice a year in the south of France. Maybe once Shawn is airborne and Bruce's tears have dried, Bruce might be a tad more receptive to a friendship with me. What do you think? Well, I'm off to the gym!

June 17

Dear Diary,

Loneliness is a lack of sense of self. This is why I fear I may always be terminally lonely.

Still, I can't help but wonder if there might be a place ... like underneath the staircase, out in the hall, in the corner, up against the wall, behind the door, up on the shelf, in the kitchen, beside the fridge next to the stove, in the closet, between some old clothes, in a book, underneath the bed, behind some boxes, out in the shed ... could there be a place where a someone like me could keep a heavy heart or leave an aching head?

In light of these new memories, I don't know who I am. I don't know who my parents were anymore. It's like when I was little and Mamma and Daddy went off and left me alone in the house for a long, long time. I feel frightened and that they left because of me. I feel like eating food, lots of food.

And these goddamned memories, which can't be my memories, are riding my back like it's the morning train. And no matter how many windows I open, I still smell oil and gasoline. I've gone through a whole bottle of Listerine and my mouth still tastes like blood. It's a tumor, I tell you. A brain tumor. There is no way that my father crawled on top of me and ... I can't even write it. I feel so guilty for imagining this.

Ruby Rae

June 24

Dear Carolyn,

I didn't get to sleep at all last night. I was out of Sominex. Funny, I've never used Sominex before in my life ... this week I used an entire box. I feel like an earthworm crawling over a razor blade.

Have you ever just hurt all over? Have you ever started crying and just couldn't stop? Have you ever been afraid to close your eyes because of what you might see?

Losing one's mind is a terrible thing, Carolyn. Last night I had this flashback and I saw Daddy crawling on top of me in the bathtub. And I felt water in my nose. I felt like I was drowning. I jumped up grabbing my throat, gasping and choking. Now, how crazy is that?

And then I remembered something about Mamma. Something, no, couldn't be ... I think I need to see them Walker brothers, Black and Red, or better yet, Jack Black or Jack Green, or maybe I should just go on down to the alley and spend the night with Little Jimmy Beam.

Doing what I have to do,
Ruby Rae

June 28

Ruby Rae, PLEASE!!!!

Even for you, you sound just too, too pathetic! Cap your jug of booze, and buy yourself some ben-wa balls! Or, at least open those *Playgirls* I sent you! There's nothing more tiresome than a drunk who's found a pen and some cheap paper. Please, do yourself and your pen pal a favor: attend an AA meeting!!!

I wish I could say something deeply intellectual. But, after your last letter, I think we'd best stay on a practical plane. As for me, I haven't heard from Bernie, so I'm going to phone him today. It's been a month since he wrote to me. Hopefully, he's had positive feedback from the *New Yorker.*

Love,
Carolyn

P.S. Just think! Only twenty-two more days till July 20th, the day I get to meet Morgan! Oh! The things that man can do with a phone! That's right, we're talking again. The naughty boy went away on business!

July 3

Dear Diary,

I've got to get out of town. Carolyn is calling Bernie about that letter I sent her to cheer her up. When Carolyn talks to Bernie ... nobody will need to buy any fireworks for the Fourth of July. But I don't care ... I'm losing my mind...

If I think my father fucked me, surely I can't be held responsible for a little forgery. Anyway, I'm busy dying. This is my swan song and it's "99 Bottles of Bourbon on the Wall."

July 4

Dear Carolyn,

Bet you never got a letter written on a cocktail napkin before. Huh? Yeah, I'm drinking at the Monkey's Foot down on Fifth Street, or is this Sixth Street, in downtown L.A.? I have friends here. They give me napkins to write you.

I found out that Winnifred was an incest expert, so to speak. I just know you think incest is beneath all my "obesity" and obsessions. But like your morals, your mind has always been in the gutter. Anyway ... fuck you. You and Kip discussing my life and treating me like an insect under a microscope. That's right.

The whole lot of you making me think my hard-working father was a pervert and a child molester and I was the child. I hate you for this. That greedy ass Winnifred ... a typical shrink ... leading me down this path ... just to get money. Great therapy. I feel worse than I did when I went in there. I oughta go put my foot in her Hebrew ass. And you ... maybe you were molested ... but don't try and drag me down into the bowels of depravity just to keep you company.

Ruby Rae ...
St. Ruby Rae to you!!!!!

July 5

Dear Carolyn,

Greetings from Betty's Pistol Dawn and Shrimp Hut, in Cudahy. You've probably never been to Cudahy. It's the poorest per capita community in America. It's south of Los Angeles ... full of Mexican gangs, white trash, drug addicts, and unwed, illiterate welfare mothers. I love it here. It's low-down and dirty just like me. Please excuse the grease on this plate. I'm out of paper and this is all I could get to write on. Did you know my father fucked me? Huh?

Did I ever tell you that? Yeah, he did. Right there in the bathtub ... and I almost drowned. I feel sick.

July 6

Dear Carolyn,

Hi, girl. I'm at the Border Motel, in San Ysidro, California. Olé! On my left there's the McDonald's where that mass murderer killed all of those people, and to my right there's Tijuana and a large order of french fries. Do you like the insects on the front of these cards? These are the state insects, like the state birds, only smaller. The snout beetle makes me lonesome for you. It's morning. I'm having a double margarita in honor of you. By now you probably know all about Bernie. Trust me, I did it for your own good.

Anyway, I'm going back to Detroit, Michigan, where the state insect is the chinch, and, girl, I'm sure gonna miss you. Yes, you heard right. I said I'm putting on my red high-heeled shoes and going back to Detroit, Michigan, where men are men and women are grateful. And I'm taking nothing with me but a paper bag full of old blue jeans and a suitcase full of blues.

I've been a fool. Kip doesn't love me. He doesn't hold me. He doesn't kiss me. He doesn't really make love to me. He's like all the rest ... nobody ever loved me. I see it all too clear now. I feel ashamed. I might as well have tattooed "Welcome" on my titties and crawled up to his bed. And speaking of beds. You know, they used to put me between them in their bed. Yeah, they did. And they used to touch me there and make me touch them there ... yeah, that's what Mommy and Daddy did.

Be seeing ya,
Ruby Rae

P.S. By the way, in case you haven't noticed, I'm taking the scenic route back to Detroit via Mexico. Could you forward this Big Mac box to Kip?

July 6

Dear Kip,

I'm going back home to Detroit, Michigan, to get me a job on the Cadillac assembly line ... 'cause you didn't love me enough. I'm sorry I had to write this on a Big Mac box ... nothing personal. Enclosed please find these fries as a token of my love.

Fuck you very much,
Ruby Rae

July 9

Dear Ruby Rae,

Thank you for your three travel-tip postcards, which arrived postage due. Gosh, I can hardly wait to make it to Betty's Pistol Dawn and Shrimp Hut. And say, I bet those double margaritas at the Border Motel are so good, you can't stop at one. Oh! By the way, how's life on the Cadillac assembly line? Even for you that was a rather too, too dramatic line, although it did firmly nail your red high heels to the cross. Now, dear, I don't want to hurt your feelings, but I really must say, you're much more pleasant when you aren't on a drunk. Snout beetle, indeed! Why don't you get lonesome for sobriety?

I hope you don't mind — I read your note to Kip. The box fell open. (You should also know our dog, Petunia, ate the fries. I'll send you the vet bill when you're solvent.) I drove to L.A. and stayed with Kip through the weekend — I offered to take him to dinner, a movie, a jazz club. But he preferred to sulk.

Kip misses you. He loves you. That he didn't love you is something you put in your head (no doubt with aid from the Brothers Christian). As for not meeting your needs, maybe Kip could have met them if you hadn't changed them every day. He said that each time he jumped through a new hoop you set up, you just gave him another hoop to jump through. Honestly, Ruby Rae! Get back to Winnifred, so you can heal enough to trust. (And, since you feel you have legitimate gripes about your relationship with Kip, why not ask him to go with you to Winnifred? Perhaps then you'll finally hear that Kip isn't at the root of the bulk of your problems.)

Granted, Kip's not the most demonstrative man (even he admits that), but all that proves is the fact he won't kiss in public because he's a devotee of Miss Manners. (And speaking of manners, just how often did you say thank you to the men who bought you drinks on your pilgrimage to the south of the border shrine of the patron saint of tequila?)

Kip wants you back; but then again, he doesn't. He's scared, Ruby Rae. He fears you'll come back only to again let Old Bush Mill and Grandad warm your belly at night. He's willing to be committed to you for life, if you're willing to get your act together.

Kip told me he doesn't want to have a marriage like Portia and Hunter's. So, I asked him, why not take her back only if she agrees to go to all her regular sessions with Winnifred, and attends AA on a daily basis? He said, "That's the way it'll have to be. A sober and reasonably sane Ruby Rae, or no reunion." And that's all there is to say.

As for me, I'm still waiting for Bernie to return my phone call. As for Morgan, I'm only eleven days away from meeting him. Oh! The anticipation that comes from waiting offers more thrills than a ride at Disneyland!

Your best friend and Soul Sister,

Carolyn

P.S. I wish I knew where to send this letter. Oh, Ruby Rae, please be all right. Please take care. Please don't wind up a statistic of the night.

VIA SPECIAL DELIVERY

July 17

Dear Carolyn,

What have I done? I've been on a two-week drunk and morphine binge. I just woke up with an empty tequila bottle under my head and a dead worm hanging from my lips in this trailer in El Rosario, Mexico. That's not even the worst of it. In my drunken stupor I married a 72-year-old, one-eyed, Mexican fish-taco peddler! He says he's 72. I think he's much older. He was married before, and I think his first wife was the woman on the old dimes. It's hot and dusty and I have the worst case of the runs I've ever had in my life and this thing I married wants to honeymoon. I'm wrecked ... totally wrecked. I have no idea how I got here. I don't remember crossing the border, meeting this man, the wedding, the blood test, nothing! I'm sure if they had really tested my blood they would've found out my blood type was bourbon and tequila. I can't believe this.

I don't know what to do. I don't have any money, or any clothes to speak of. Girl, I'm wearing a pair of spider-strap spikes, some mesh hose, a teddy, a polyester t-shirt dress with a picture of Benito Juárez on the front and Montezuma on the back, and my hair was pulled back in a bun, with dead flowers in it. This just can't be. He said this was my wedding dress. That and a veil. To add insult to injury the veil wasn't even white ... it was bone!

There's no phone in this joint, nothing. No television, no radio, just a bunch of books written in Spanish and the tackiest collection of statues of saints and Jesus you've ever seen. I hope you get this letter. It took me an entire day to get him to understand that I needed a stamp. Every time I'd say stamp ... he'd stomp his feet and look at me with that one eye, grin like a toothless Cheshire cat, and rub his crotch.

Carolyn, you've got to help me. I know that this is asking a lot, but when you get this letter you've got to tell Kip that

I was kidnapped by the Moonies and forced to write that note to him at gunpoint in a McDonald's bathroom ... and I'm being held hostage in one of their camps. Remember, I nursed you back to health when you were down. Granted, I didn't speak to you, and you don't have to speak to me now either. But, girl, you've got to help me!

Get on the first plane that's flying closest to El Rosario and come and get me. You can write to me at: 2 El Calle De Mayor, El Rosario, Baja California, Mexico. Oh, I'm known here by the name of Lucia Mendoza. Don't ask ... you don't want to know.

Please, Carolyn ... you've got to help me. You've got to. Remember your operation ... I helped you. And I did the best I could with the dust ... I really did. Please ... please. And please tell Kip that I was captured by the Moonies. Please, Carolyn ... please. You're my only hope ... please.

At your mercy,
Ruby Rae

WESTERN UNION TELEGRAM

SENORA LUCIA MENDOZA
2 EL CALLE DE MAYOR
EL ROSARIO MEXICO

JULY 18 STOP SINCE THE FLOWERS IN YOUR HAIR DIED ON YOUR WEDDING NIGHT THINGS MUST NOT BE ALL BAD STOP BUT I'LL COME ANYWAY STOP WILL ARRIVE BY PLANE ON THE 20TH THE DAY I HAD PLANNED TO MEET MORGAN STOP BETTER BE OVER JIM BEAM AND ALL THOSE OTHER MEN OR I WON'T LEND YOU ANY DINERO FOR KAOPECTATE STOP IF YOU JOINED AA YOU WOULDN'T BE IN THIS MESS STOP CAROLYN STOP THIS BETTER BE A REAL EMERGENCY STOP YOU KNOW I HATE TO FLY STOP A FISH MONGER'S WIFE REALLY MY DEAR STOP

UNITED WRITERS' AGENCY
From the Desk of
BERNARD GOLDSTEIN

July 18

Dear Ms. Spencer,

While your story "The Pond in the Silver Winter" shows merit and potential, I don't feel that you are ready to compete in the realm of professional writers at this time.

Please feel free to contact me if there are further developments in your career.

Best wishes,
Bernard Goldstein

BG/fk

VIA SPECIAL DELIVERY

July 23

Dear, dear Lucia
(or do you prefer the more formal Senora Mendoza?),

I've got good news and bad news. And for you, the news is mostly bad. I'm here in Ensenada at Magdalena Goldberg's Hacienda, Panderia, and Tax Service (first fifteen minutes free with proof of bakery purchase at the Panderia). That I'm in a room with concrete-block walls painted a very lime shade of green doesn't really matter, because, well, let's just say, the all of me has been rather occupied. With a man. A real man. He used to smoke Camels, but he still wears a lumberjack's shirt. And, speaking of clothes, for the past seventy-two hours I've only worn a bumper sticker that reads, "I love Hussong's Long Bar Cantina" (and I do love Hussong's long bar, and I do mean long bar). Isn't life grand? I'm loving this. All of it. Even the *cinco-peso* champagne that my passionate conquistador poured into ... well ... the only thing that matters is that my new beau is my dream come true. He's Bruce gone straight. I'm in a state of beyond-lust! It's just too heavenly! Thanks ever so much for causing me to break my date with Morgan. In fact, I'm so grateful, I'll even overlook that little stunt you pulled with Bernie. (Now, all you have to do is hope that Bernie will also be so magnanimous.)

Anyway, I know I was supposed to be at your place three days ago. I suspect my unannounced delay caused you some headaches. I'm sorry for that. If you thought I was dead, I'm sure you had my funeral planned. Oh, well, just save the plans with the thought they'll come in handy after we next meet again.

I bet you're just dying to know all about my new man! WELL! We sat side by side on the plane. Once we were airborne, and my palms puddled over with nervous perspiration, he did his best to cure me of my fear of flying.

(You did read that book *Fear of Flying*, didn't you? If you did, let me just say, after three days of this bliss I can write its sequel.) And once he cured my fear of flying ... well ... it only seemed right that I let him go on to curing other, more important things.

I telegraphed Rick. I told him not to expect me back. It'd be too cruel to tell him about my new lover, Conrad, so I just said I was headed to Cabos San Lucas to think things over. That's right, my dear. You read it correctly the first time. Cabos San Lucas. Conrad has a little diving business down there, and he's arranged for me to rent a villa near his for the season! Doesn't that sound just too, too divine? Isn't this just too, too romantic?

Now, not to worry! I haven't forgotten about your little dilemma with your 72-year-old husband and his unpleasant nuptial demands. Between inventing two new sexual positions and dashing down to Consuela's Magic Comb (torrid sex just doesn't do a thing for my hair — when I'm with a real man, it always gets matted in the back), I managed to buy, and enclose, a cashier's check (or whatever it is that they call it down here) made out to Lucia Mendoza in the amount equal to one thousand U.S. dollars. This should be all you need to get out of your little jam.

Once you've said *adios* to your husband, do yourself some favors. Make an appointment with Winnifred, sign up at the nearest AA, and give Kip a call. He looks like death (and sounds worse) since you left. (Plus, from what you write, the separation hasn't done much to improve your lot.) Kip provides you with a sense of stability, which you just can't seem to provide yourself. — Besides, since you love each other, why not lean on your relationship while you recover from your fling with Jim Beam?

I'll write from Cabos San Lucas (Thank God I kept in shape with aerobics and can fit into one of those sexy, low-cut, one-piece swimsuits!) If there's a wedding, you can be my bridesmaid.

Sorry for not being there for you! But I'm sure the enclosed funds will ease your disappointment.

Carolyn

P.S. While life has proven that I have no talent for children, writing, or marriage, it has proved I am an ace when it comes to landing a man. It shouldn't take me more than six months to close this deal.

July 24

Dear Carolyn,

You are a worthless, no-good, low-down, morally depraved, capricious, wayward, mindless, man-hungry, clitoris-governed, penis-driven joy beast from the east side of hell! (And these are just the compliments.) How dare you? You goddamned lust hound. I know you're upset about Morgan, and I know you were livid about Bernie, but haven't you heard about the HIV virus? If you get sick as the result of this little tryst, I'm not going to take care of you.

How fucking dare you! I told you that I had nothing but a teddy, a pair of spikes, and a t-shirt dress almost as tacky as you are. Just how did you expect me to cash a cashier's check made out to Lucia Mendoza? Huh? Huh? I don't believe you ... committing adultery with this man on the plane and running off with him ... stone cold sober ... you're a tramp, Carolyn. And if you marry this one, which I know you will, you oughta wear a Hefty Bag to the altar, 'cause you're trash, Carolyn ... do you hear me? Trash. Are you getting a kickback from Uncle Ben's Rice Company?

Let me tell you what happened as a result of your little tryst. I finally had to give in to my husband's matrimonial demands and he died on top of me! That's right, Carolyn, while you're off playing Amelia Airhead, I was prying Bosco's arms from around my neck. I had to walk five blocks in spikes to get an ambulance. Of course, it was too late. It was too late when I met him.

Anyway, the mortician was nice enough to cash your cashier's check for me and I was able to get out of there and back home. Kip hasn't come home yet to find me here ... we'll see what happens.

Screw you,
Ruby Rae

P.S. You're only a failure with marriage and writing ... if you quit trying. As for children ... who cares?

July 28

Dear Widow Mendoza,

Condolences, doll. Such a loss, at such an early age. As for me, life is just too glorious. I look just too, too fabu with a tan. Course, you wouldn't know anything about that. Just kidding, my dear. Conrad's the everything I've ever wanted in a man. He's kind, gentle, sensitive, and in tune with his feelings. He's very verbal, has a good sense of self-worth, and great hands. Oh! His wonderful, wonderful hands!!! They give the very best back and other rubs. And last night he just held and held me! I swear, it's heaven to walk on the beach with a man who can hold your hand and talk at the same time.

I hope we're still friends, Ruby Rae. I hope you aren't too upset with me. I'm glad you're back with Kip. I hope you've seen Winnifred. Write soon!

I miss you,
Carolyn

P.S. Do you truly think my short story was really, really bad?

P.P.S. As for Rick, I'll drop him a note in the next few days. I'm not quite sure what I'll say. He wasn't a bad husband. He just wasn't there for me in some basic way. I think he liked me, but I don't think he loved me.

As he supported me while I wrote, I'll tell him to keep the twenty-five thousand dollars I put down on the house. I'll also mail him my great-grandmother's canary diamond that I wore as a wedding ring (during this, as well as my second marriage). The two-karat gem was appraised at forty-five grand. I'll tell him he can sell it to get reimbursed for the rest of the expenses I incurred while living with him.

August 9

Dear Carolyn,

Kip has been a total dear, and he's being very supportive of me. I haven't told him everything. I mean about being married to Bosco Mendoza and having him die on top of me and all.

I went to my first AA meeting. I told them about the terrible things that happened to me and they didn't bat an eye. It was a very trying experience to raise my hand when they said, "Are there any other alcoholics in the room?" and everybody raised their hands. I hate thinking of myself as an alcoholic. When I think of alcoholics, I think of desperate winos down on skid row ... and it ain't me ... I think of sad actresses isolated in their room with a bottomless whiskey glass ... and it ain't me ... I think a lot of things, but none of them are me.

I'm an alcoholic, Carolyn. As much pain as alcohol caused me in my childhood, it's a painful irony for me to realize that I grew up to be a boozer; a boozer like my mamma coming home drunk, eating canned goods mixed with eggs and then puking it all over the floor; drunk like my daddy, sitting in total darkness, save the lit end of a cigarette, at the dining room table, listening to the same John Lee Hooker song over and over. It's painful, Carolyn.

And speaking of painful, Carolyn. It's painful for me to watch you throw your life away like this. You're a man junkie ... better yet, an altar junkie. Why don't you go to the altar with yourself? I don't mean to be cold and I don't mean to be arrogant or presumptuous and I don't mean to "take your inventory," that's something they say in program ... but anyway, I think you're looking for something in these men that you can't ever find. I think you're looking to find something that Hunter couldn't give you many years ago. I think you're going to have to face up to the reality, Carolyn, that it just didn't happen the way you wanted it to. That's what I'm learning here.

Funny, I joined Overeaters Anonymous too, and without food and booze to stuff down my feelings, all of these feelings are coming up.

I love you,
Ruby Rae

P.S. I think your short story is fine and if you don't mind ... as a peace offering for my dastardly deed, which was well intended, I'd like to send it to an editor at a quarterly magazine that publishes a lot of short stories.

August 13

Dear Ruby Rae,

I appreciate your concern, dear, but people in glass houses shouldn't throw stones. You drink yourself into oblivion, and wake up married to a recent escapee from the geriatric ward who reeks of fish. Then, as if that isn't bad enough, you kill him with your cantaloupe-through-the-eye-of-a-needle trick. Now, you tell me who most needs our concern, you bigamist! I may have been married a number of times, but I have never been married to more than one man at a time!

Unlike you, I don't view myself as an altar junkie. I view my multi-marriages like the rings on the trunk of a tree: they're growth marks. As I mature, I just expand. Sometimes, I even send off another shoot that moves my roots elsewhere. For an intelligent, evolving person like me, sometimes change just has to be.

I'm pleased you joined AA and OA. I'm pleased things are going well with Kip. You were wise to go back to him. But don't tell him about your Mexico experience.

Conrad has taken me to live on Cloud Nine. His boat wasn't booked this morning, so we snorkeled. Then, we had a romantic hour in a secluded cove. I've discovered the free feeling of swimming nude!

I've written Rick two letters that explain what happened. I hope my words sink through his thick skull. I hope he regrets not giving me a wedding ring, or getting coverage on the day we married. I hope he regrets never taking me on a honeymoon. I hope he feels as alone as I ever did when I lived with him. I hope he feels ashamed when he receives my great-grandmother's canary diamond ring.

Write soon. And send any and all scoop you have about Rick, and how he's adjusted to my little trip! Now that I'm gone, he may appreciate me.

My love to you and Kip!
Carolyn

P.S. Regarding my short story, I know you were well intentioned. Do whatever you want with it. For all I care, you can tear it up and feed it to Winnifred's fish.

August 20

Dear Carolyn,

I'm happy that you're happy. I really am, and I didn't mean to offend you. I was just expressing my opinion. Perhaps your many wedding rings are just like rings on a tree: growth marks. And perhaps my stretch marks are just growth marks. I suppose, if I wanted to view them that way. If nothing else, at least now I understand all of those grooves in your left-hand ring finger.

Yes, I could fight with you and take this stance or that ... but I'm just too weak from my feelings. I'm just too god-damned weak. I hurt all over. There have been days when I just had to lie in my bed and cry all day long. I just can't help taking those trips down memory lane ... way on down memory lane back to Slag Alley in the bathroom with Daddy, me and him taking a bath and then him on top of me and, oh, God, Carolyn. Oh, God ... I'm just so angry. I want to go and piss on his grave. I want to go and dig his bones up and shit in his skull. I want to grind his bones with my foot against the pavement until they're bone meal and then fertilize the flowers on the lawn of the KKK headquarters ... only because I know it would kill him all over again.

No wonder I was a drunk and a Big Mac junkie ... no wonder ... no fucking wonder. It's just too painful when I realize that the only time my father ever held me in his arms was to fuck me. That's right, Carolyn ... that's my big, deep, dark secret ... not that he molested me ... but that the only time he ever held me in his arms, the only time he ever kissed me, was while he was fucking me ... yes ... that's what happened.

And then there were all of those nights him and Mamma pulled me in the bed between them and ... I just can't write about it. Why Carolyn? Why me? It hurts so much. Sometimes, I think I'm just going to double over and die from the pain. You know, I hear dogs die from broken hearts. Well, I'm feeling like a big dog ... and if I do die ... please don't let them cremate me, 'cause I've been burned enough in this life.

And the worse of it is that I went around all of those years harboring that pain and humiliation and I wasn't even aware of it. I can see Daddy sitting on the porch with the other men, boasting about how spoiled I was as I rode by on my brand-new bicycle with the memory of him and Mamma clawing its way out of my head. Oh, I'm so goddamned angry. This is like being raped forty, no, fifty, no, five hundred times in a row and never having the opportunity to even shower or wipe the intruders' slobber off your lips. I hate him, Carolyn ... and I hate her too. They're lucky that they're dead. They're goddamned lucky that they're dead or I'd go and put a bullet through their heads.

But enough of the bad things ... I can see in color again ... I didn't realize that everything had faded to black-and-white until the other day when I got the letter from my friend at the magazine and noticed her stationery had four different colors on it.

Which brings me to the good news. They bought your short story for $150.00 ... Congrats. Now the bad news is I've had a little relapse and gone on a shopping binge and spent the money. Just kidding ... I've enclosed your check ... it's not forged, I swear!!!

As for Rick, he's been calling me. He suspects that there is someone else and that I had something to do with all of it. He's heartbroken ... or ego-broken. I'm tempted to give him those letters that you wrote to me about that gay man in the lighting and fabric store so he can know just how lonely you were. I think I will the next time he calls ... if it's okay with you. Well, I gotta go and get ready for an AA meeting.

One day at a time...
Ruby Rae

P.S. I don't smell oil and gasoline anymore ... well only at the gas station. That's right, I can pump my own gas ... I've come a long way, baby!

August 24

Ruby Rae,

I hope you enjoy these flowers, and they don't remind you of the flowers you recently woke up to find in your hair. (I had a hell of a time finding a florist who does business on an "international" level.)

Thanks ever so much for selling my story. If anybody was in need of an ego boost I was. Also, a big congratulations on sticking it out with Winnifred. But don't go overboard with the gas thing. Now that you've conquered the beast, you deserve to pull into a full-serve station. (Oh, and now that you're seeing in color again, I guess you plan to do something about the color — if you can call it that — of your kitchen.)

As for what's happening south of the border, Conrad and I had quite the romantic time last night. An hour before sunset, we walked to the beach with a sack of shellfish. We gathered wood between kisses. We built a tremendous bonfire. The crab and lobster baked while we drank a bottle of wonderful German wine. After dinner, we crawled beneath our blanket. We talked, and laughed, and held each other till dawn. We returned to his villa, all sandy and cold, and jumped into the shower. I half expected him to ask me to move in with him as we stood under the spray's warmth. I mean, we're not together all the time, but we spend enough evenings together that shared rent is a reasonable consideration. We have such great times, and sex is uncontrolled in a terrific way, if you know what I mean. Why shouldn't we live together so we can partake of this pleasure whenever we like? Personally, I don't think this deal down here should be difficult to close. When I told Conrad that Rick didn't give me a wedding ring he tore off a beer can ring and slipped it on my finger. — If that's not an expression of serious interest, I don't know what is.

I think I'll wait a few weeks before I drop hints to Conrad about consolidating our addresses. It's not like he's dating anyone else. Granted, he does have an ex-girlfriend, Theresa, down here. (Conrad rarely speaks of her except to say he hated the way she never cleaned her hair out of his brush after she borrowed it.) But they broke up six months ago. That's more than enough time for a heart to mend. Plus, their relationship couldn't have been all that great, since it barely survived a year of living together.

I haven't heard from Rick, have you? I write him every day, and my address heads the letters. Perhaps the Mexico mail system is as bad as they say. But if I've received all of your letters, why haven't I received his? I guess Rick never did really, deep, deep down, love me. If he did, he'd come after me. Or at least write.

Send me your honest assessment of my situation. I'm sure I can still go back to Rick. Like you, I haven't told my husband about the other man in the picture. I wish you could hug me, so I'd know you still love me.

Carolyn

P.S. If you think it'll do some good, send Rick my letters about my in-lust experience with Bruce. It might give Rick a better perspective on our relationship than my direct letters to him have. Thanks!

August 31

Dear Carolyn,

I wish I could hug you, too. You sound like you're searching so hard. So very hard. I'm very impressed with how you've been able to deal with your incest issues and go on with your life. And it's not for me to judge how many husbands you have had ... not for me at all ... I guess everything is how it's supposed to be and when I criticize it, I guess I'm saying that I know better than God. So I'm learning acceptance. I'm learning to take the good from life and to take the bad and hold them at equal heights in equal hands and look at them both straight on and see how much they are truly alike. I will always love you, Carolyn, for the many things that you have given me and done for me over the months. I'm grateful for the $1000 that you sent me in a cashier's check; it was more than you were obliged to do. I'm grateful for all of these letters that we've been able to share. I'm grateful for all of the support and encouragement that you've given me over the past months ... I really am grateful for the dark parts of your life that you shared with me, because that darkness brought me into the light in many ways. And believe me, I really love you.

Now down to the next issue: Rick. I had already sent him your letters about that lighting and fabric store queen when I asked your permission. He's angry, he's hurt, he's confused ... and rightfully so. How would you feel if you put him on a plane and he just didn't come home and the plane didn't crash? Come on, Carolyn...

I know you love Rick. It's in your letters ... all of your letters. You wouldn't fret so over his attention if you didn't. I just hope he's there when you get back. I hope he's as understanding and wonderful as Kip was about my foolish leaving. Of course, I was drunk ... what's your excuse?

And you know what else I wonder? I wonder if you want Hunter to come and save you from that uncle ... and if by doing this whole thing you're not recreating your incest experience to try and work it out. Maybe you're not as over your incest issues as you think.

By the way, Kip and I are going to see Winnifred together.

Your sister,
Ruby Rae

September 4

Dear Ruby Rae,

Alcoholism's a disease, not a lifelong excuse for fucking up. Sorry, that was mean. I'm jealous you're in a growth spurt at a time when I'm not. I'm also envious Kip is willing to see Winnifred. Rick would never go to marriage counseling. (He claimed he hadn't the time.) In many ways, you've made wiser relationship decisions than I've made. You've structured your relationship with Kip in a way that allows for expansion and personal growth. None of my relationships have ever had built-in "stretchability," so I had to leave them when I sought change. I don't know. I've begun to wonder if I'm too fucked up to be in any relationship, much less a healthy one. Maybe Rick and Mike and Chris and Josh weren't the real problem. Maybe I was, and still am.

I agree with your comments about Rick. He has every reason to be angry. I violated his trust. I walked because it was easy. I behaved like a six-year-old who abandons her friend when another classmate offers her a bigger piece of candy. (And speaking of children, I'm finally over Molly.)

On top of this, I'm sure Rick is sick of my complaints. I bitched and screamed that he was tuning me out and pushing me away. Then he'd be hurt, and would push me even further away. After five years, I got pissed and swung out with a king-sized shove. Only, I'm unsure I intended it to be the shove that'd end our marriage.

I don't understand the part of me that's so tied to Rick. Perhaps he'll be more receptive to me after he reads my letters to you about Bruce. Maybe then he'll write, and his words will help me sort though my feelings.

Now that I've had my first sale, I think I want to start working on my manuscript again. Would you be a dear and get it from Rick?

Thanks for sticking by me,
Carolyn

P.S. Rick in the role of Hunter, who I want to save me from an uncle, who dresses in the guise of Conrad?! Honey, please! I think you saw Winnifred an hour too long this week! Even Freud knew that sometimes a cigar is just a cigar! (Or haven't you ever had one of those dreams?)

September 7

Dear Carolyn,

Just a quick note, I'm out the door. Rick called and said that he and a friend are coming to Los Angeles in the next week. I couldn't get anything out of him on the phone, but he said that he would talk to me when he got down here. I must admit I wasn't really in the mood to talk. I'm going through some really difficult times in therapy. I don't feel like going into it now.

Ruby Rae

September 8

Dear Diary,

I know this is going to sound strange. Today, for the first time in my life, I peed standing up. It's the strangest thing ... all of these years, I've thought of myself as a woman. But the fact of the matter is I'm a man ... biologically. The mind is so much stronger than the body ... and the world the body lives in. I've gone through my whole life believing that I was a woman.

All of my business associates, my best friends, everybody, except Kip, who considers me to be a she with a dick, thinks I'm a woman.

But I'm not a woman, whatever that is. I'm a man, whatever that is. Hmmm, ain't this peculiar? Never a dull moment. And if Mother Mary Timothy thought she was shocked to find me on the altar with Steve's penis in my mouth, imagine what she would've done if she'd pulled my dress up and found out the real truth. Can you imagine how shocked she would have been to find out she was training a man to be a nun?

Ruby Rae

September 8

Ruby Rae,

I have just suffered through my all-time worst case of dyspepsia. If you have any cash, buy stock in Tums. After the business I gave them today, their income for this quarter has skyrocketed.

You have no idea of what I had to endure for breakfast. It was worse than those pancakes you make for Kip that are always runny in the middle. It was worse than that cake you baked for Hunter just before he died (no association intended).

Anyhow, the worst thing about my case of gas is that it wasn't caused by food, so I can't upchuck. It was caused by a woman. The woman who served the food. That's right. THE woman. Theresa. Conrad's ex. She's a waitress who doesn't even have the good sense to clear and serve plates from the correct sides.

God only knows what Conrad ever saw in her. She has mousey brown hair, and mousey brown eyes, and a mousey disposition. She moves about like a knock-kneed rodent adorned with the long, droopy ears of a lop-eared rabbit. Then, to top it off, she was as nice (of course, she's nice. Those types can't be anything but nice) and as polite to me as one of those kids working at Disneyland. That's right, doll. She called me ma'am. To add insult to injury, Conrad followed her every move with adoring eyes. (He claimed he wouldn't have taken me to the Cafe Jamón Sur Del Mar had he known that she had a new job there.)

Ruby Rae, I haven't the foggiest idea what Conrad ever saw in her. Unless, of course, well — it might have been — it must have been, for sex. They do say that some of those mousey types are tigers in bed. But then, when it comes to tigers, I'm queen of the pride, so why should I be worried?

As soon as we left the Cafe Jamón Sur Del Mar, Conrad was hot to trot and ready to roll (if you know what I mean), so we had a quickie in a narrow breezeway that was strong with the scent from the next-door fish store (my thoughts briefly turned toward your ex). I haven't done anything so deliciously risqué since my second husband and I did the deed on the bleachers at his high school's football field. (Men! They always let the little head speak for the big head. But then, that's why women are so much more evolved than them.)

Feeling better now that I've written.

Love you,
Carolyn

September 11

Dear Diary,

I just got back from therapy. I hate therapy. Every day that I go there I come home with some worse news about myself. Today, I learned that in order to be truly on a path of healing, I have to be honest with everyone about my gender.

Now how am I going to explain this to Carolyn? Carolyn, who would be a dyke in a second if women had dicks, or longer, thicker tongues. Did I say that? Oh, well ... it's a program of rigorous honesty. I can see it now ... "Oh, by the way, Carolyn, I have good news and bad news. The good news is you're finally at the place in your recovery where you can trust a man ... the bad news is I'm the man and I've been deceiving you all these months ... So back to the drawing board."

Ruby Rae

VIA SPECIAL DELIVERY

September 11

Dear Ruby Rae,

I just got your news about Rick coming to L.A. — the Mexican mail can be soooo slow. I bet he's stopping at your place on his way down here to get me. I bet he's bringing his friend for moral and physical support. Trés romantique! Trés romantique! What shall I wear for the Big Day? This vacation has done wonders for my looks, so Rick will like what he sees. Do I sound like a vain Mrs. Doctor, or what?

After I got your letter, I realized I've had unrealistic expectations for my relationships with men. I want them to be my lovers, my confidants, and my very best friends. But no man can ever be all that. I mean, look at our relationship. We would never have such a close friendship if you were a man. Men can't handle intimacy. If they could, they'd socialize with one another around something other than sports activities.

Accepting this has enabled me to lower my expectations for a love relationship. Since men are incapable of being what I need them to be for me, I'll take my needs that husband can't fulfill to you, and my other women friends. If I do this, my marriage will be more sane.

Be a dear and telegraph me when Rick and his friend leave for Cabos San Lucas. I'll encourage Conrad to work or go out with a friend on the day of their expected arrival. When Conrad comes back, he'll return to a Dear John letter. Don't worry, I'll let him down gently. I've had lots of experience with breakups.

Thanks for everything! Thanks especially for coming up with the just too fabulous idea of showing Rick my letters to you about Bruce! The best thing I ever did was to fall in lust with that too wonderful and delightful man!

I love you oodles and oodles! You're the best friend I've ever had!

Carolyn

P.S. Instead of the Dear John letter, I'll just suggest to Conrad that he take Theresa snorkeling. (Of course, with her ears she'll probably get caught in a kelp bed and drown.) I'll just say that after I saw the way they eyed each other in the restaurant, they ought to see if they still have feelings for each other. I can be so generous with my men!

September 12

Dear Diary,

I'm preparing for Rick's visit. I don't know whether or not to tell him yet. These doctors are so dense when it comes to transvestism, homosexuality, and incest abuse. They tend to just throw everything in one big pot and say they're all a result of each other. I'm not a transvestite because of incest, and being gay has nothing to do with wearing dresses or having slept with my parents. Granted everything in this universe is interrelated, but not necessarily interdependent. But trying to explain that to a doctor ... they hate being taught. I guess too many years of being taught the wrong way. I've always felt sorry for doctors. People expect them to be God, so they act like God and believe they're God, and when they inevitably fail, because they're not God, they're condemned for not being God, and sued for trying. Hmmmm. When an overweight black drag queen pities your estate in life ... you're in trouble.

Ruby

September 14

Dear Carolyn,

Dear, dear Carolyn. Girl, sit down. If you're sitting down, lay down. Honey, where do I start? How about the head? Rick has streaked his hair, pierced his ear, bought some (blue-violet) designer contacts, dropped the "c," and added a second "k" and placed a vowel at the end of his name. It's now Rikki with an "i." Yes, and Rikki has had the diamond in your wedding band from your second marriage turned into a pinky ring ... and that lighting and fabric store queen is wearing it! Read 'em and weep. Rikki went to the City to talk to that queen about getting in touch with his male sensitivity and, well ... that queen showed him a thing or three that got Rick in touch with his sensitive spot. Honey, Rikki traded in your dog, Petunia, for two poodles ... Alexis and Crystal.

And, yes, that lighting and fabric store queen was able to make Rikki understand the damaging effects the rigors of a surgeon's life can have on a relationship. So your husband retired from practice and opened a notions boutique in Shawn's old art studio, called "Miss Rikki's Knit and Sew." That's right, doll. Your man is selling buttons and yarn, honey ... is that sensitive enough for you?

Girlfriend, they busted in here wearing enough cologne to drown out the smell of all the fisheries in Ensenada, and I know you smelled the fisheries in Ensenada on your way to Hussong's. And Rikki was not coming to L.A. to find out about you exactly. What he said was that he wanted to know some things about you ... and what he wanted to know was where you kept your furs in storage. And, like you said to me, condolences, doll ... such a loss at such an early age. That man didn't want to get back in your life, he just wanted to get back in your closet.

The real reason they were coming to L.A. was to go dancing at "Outrage," this gay bar in West Hollywood. What can I say? I know it must be painful losing your man to your masturbation fantasy. I guess you just let that lighting and fabric store queen into your bedroom one too many times...

I'll be here,
Ruby Rae

P.S. There is some good news in all of this: Rikki gave me your manuscript. He said with what he and Bruce have done "motif-wise" with your ex-boudoir, there is absolutely no room for any of your writing, or writing paraphernalia ... see attached box ... (the jungle vine takes up all of the room ... I guess I forgot to tell you, Bruce calls Rikki "Jungle Beast" ... perhaps you should've put your creativity to work and come up with a similar nickname and matching motif for Rick, I mean Rikki). Again, condolences, doll.

September 14

Dear Diary,

Rikki was here with his new gay lover. Funny, I guess technically I'm a gay man. I don't feel like a gay man. I didn't feel like I was one of them. They seemed like men to me, and I seemed like a woman. I can't help but wonder ... what's a woman ... what's a man? You know I don't know if I could ever wear "men's clothes" ... they're so unfestive.

Anyway, I decided not to tell him my gender. I was too busy trying to find some Dramamine so I could watch him swish around my house.

Ruby Rae

September 17

Dear Ruby Rae,

This is a fine example of what happens when people like you offer advice that's actually listened to! How could I place my entire future in the hands of an ex-drunk and reformed bigamist? Well, if nothing else, I'm now certain all the fish I've eaten down here were spawned over nuclear waste drums.

Now, you listen to me, Mzzzz. Ruby Rae Senora Lucia Mendoza! And you listen, but good!! You are to go up to our — my — house on MacQuiddy Lake. You are to go into my house and rip down every one of those tacky drapes, which you'll then put in my canoe and dump in the middle of my lake! — And you better be sure they're dumped, Senora Mendoza! I'll spill the beans to Kip about your detour to El Rosario if I discover any part of any of those drapes doing for you what drapes once did for Miss Scarlett O'Hara! (Besides dear, you haven't her figure!)

Yes! I am in a mood! But what else could you expect? None of my husbands have ever dumped me! Much less dumped me for a man! At least, icky Rick(i) could have had the courtesy to dump me for some blonde bimbette, rather than my very own, hand-picked lust-object! How dare Rick steal my very own stud from under me, so to speak?! It's just so like a man to do something like this! They're so deceitful! I hate them!

The biggest mistake of my life was taking Rick to bake bread with Bruce! I can't believe the nerve of that — that — that — muslin sissy! He swiped my husband, my great-grandmother's $45,000 canary diamond ring, and my best recipe! Well! You can be damned sure I'll see to it that man hands me back my prize-winning recipe! And you can be damned sure I'll let him keep Rick(i)! — As for the diamond ring, I'll make him think it carries a curse that'll make all his muscles permanently flaccid. I am livid, Ruby Rae. Livid! And when I return home, I'm marching into San Francisco's gay church and demanding they return my last two years of very hefty donations!

As for you, you ex-nun-in-training: you'd best break out your rosary beads and pray fast and hard to St. Jude that I'm able to get my Conrad back! It's not every day that I discard a perfectly good man to a modest violet with a rabbit's lopped ears who's "nice."

Hating ALL MEN MORE THAN EVER BEFORE!!!!!!

Carolyn

September 17

Dear Diary,

Rikki isn't doing anything to help me break the news to Carolyn that I'm a man. Winnifred says that I shouldn't worry about Carolyn right now, I should start with some other people in my life.

Ruby

September 21

Carolyn,

I would gladly go up to your house on MacQuiddy Lake and get down all of those drapes that you bought except Rikki and Bruce are on an extended honeymoon in the Orient, and some big bald-headed guy dripping with leather and chains named Toddy is taking care of the place. I hear from Meg that he's real tidy and everybody on MacQuiddy Lake is impressed with how he's brought out your impatiens and snapdragons. I must admit they do look quite lovely. Besides, didn't you tell Rick he could keep the house? And the ring? Wasn't that a part of the divorce settlement?

Now, Carolyn, I know that you're upset and I can understand your wanting to take back your donations to the gay church (or my making racist and anti-Semitic remarks whenever I get angry with Shelly or Winnifred) ... but isn't that a bit like the liberal who believes in integration until the blacks move next door and start cooking ribs? I mean queens love men, and they take men from women all the time, and the first time you lose a man to a queen you're on the Anita Bryant bandwagon. Just because you were lying up there in your bed, dreaming about being a cat on that fabric store queen's lap and waiting for him to pour you a saucer of milk ... when the truth of the matter is the only thing you could do for him was surrender your husband ... which you did, I might add. Well, how's the milk, doll? Just in case that queen didn't send you the milk, I'm taking this opportunity to send you this carton ... and since this is a memorable occasion ... I splurged and got half 'n' half ... which says it all. Now if you were really in the spirit of things, you would let it separate and drink the skim and send the cream to that queen ... Wear your curtains, indeed!

Furthermore, how dare you threaten me with telling Kip the whole story! I'm really disappointed in you ... again. After all, wasn't it I who told you all along you were doing the wrong thing, and would you listen to me? Nooooo!

Trying to talk sense into you is like trying to get Annette Funicello to retire.

Clean and Sober,
Ruby Rae

P.S. By the way, when Meg wasn't looking Molly gave me this enclosed note for you.

Dear Carelin,
My mommy says you can play wif me she doesnt like me. she doesnt give me the bestedest cookies or toys. Come soone love Molly

September 24

Dear Meg,

I just received the enclosed letter from Molly at my villa in Cabos San Lucas. Perhaps now you'll understand that it was your daughter, and not me, who was trying to pit us against one another. Molly would draw me into her life, and then once she had my full attention, she'd get me to do things for her that you forbid. Then, she'd step back and watch the fireworks between us.

In light of this, perhaps you'll read my enclosed letter to Molly.

Carolyn

September 24

Dear Molly,

I now live in Mexico, so I can't come out and play with you. Your mommy loves you a great deal. She doesn't buy you the bestest cookies because cookies have sugar, and sugar is bad for you. She doesn't buy you the bestest toys because if you got the bestest toys every time you asked for them, you wouldn't know the pleasure of looking forward to receiving something special.

I know your mommy doesn't seem like a friend, but mommies aren't put on this earth to only be friends. There are lots of other important things mommies also have to do, like teach their children manners, and make sure they do their homework, and keep their rooms tidy, and eat their vegetables. Since your mommy does all these things (and more), you should be thankful you have a good mommy. This is a lot more than many children have in this world.

Because you have a good mommy, I'm going to tell you a special secret. You shouldn't do things behind her back, like writing to tell me she said I can see you. I can't see you, because she doesn't want me to see you. And we have to respect that. Because being a good mommy is what your mommy does best.

Goodbye,
Carolyn

WESTERN UNION TELEGRAM

TO RUBY RAE STONE

SEPTEMBER 24 STOP WE AREN'T EVER EVER EVER EVER SPEAKING STOP AND YOU KNOW WHY STOP SO DON'T EVEN BOTHER TO ASK STOP AND DON'T EVER MENTION THE WORD MAN TO ME STOP I HATE THEM STOP ALL OF THEM STOP THEY'RE EITHER SPINELESS WONDERS STOP HEARTBREAKERS STOP CHILD MOLESTERS STOP OR COWARDS DRESSED IN THE GUISE OF BULLIES STOP WE SHOULD FREEZE ALL THEIR SPERM AND THEN RID THE PLANET OF THEM AND THE REST OF THE COCKROACHES STOP CAROLYN P.S. HOW DARE YOU TAKE RICK(I)'S SIDE STOP DON'T YOU KNOW WOMEN HAVE TO STICK TOGETHER STOP HOW WOULD YOU FEEL IF KIP RAN OFF WITH BOSCO MENDOZA AND I WROTE BACK ABOUT YOUR FORMER SNAPDRAGONS STOP

September 24

Dear Diary,

Well, I took Winnifred's advice and told my agent I was a man. He dropped me. This ain't no fun at all.

Ruby Rae

October 3

Okay, fine, Ruby Rae!

Be like that! Don't grovel for my forgiveness. Don't be concerned about my mental health now that I'm manless. If you hadn't written about Rick(i) coming down, I never would have kissed off Conrad. I only suggested he take Theresa snorkeling. I never expected him to actually ask her to marry him. That's right, doll. You've provided me with an opportunity to be a bridesmaid. Indeed, it's my first opportunity to be a bridesmaid. Her only bridesmaid (the good news is, the odds favor my catching her bouquet). Oh, did I tell you that the bridesmaid's dress is a very lime shade of green? The last time I was near this particular shade, I was wearing only a bumper sticker. Touché.

Thanks for going on a binge that placed me on a path which enabled me to lose everything important in my life. (And, on top of all of this, I now have to buy a wedding gift, and it isn't even for me.)

HATING ALL MEN MORE THAN I EVER THOUGHT POSSIBLE!!!!!!

Carolyn

P.S. Thanks for the letter from Molly.

October 5

Dear Diary,

I got a letter from Carolyn. I wish I could answer it. But all she mostly talks about is how she hates men. I don't need this. I'm really close to the edge. I feel like crossing the River Styx, I really do. Maybe it's an easier world over there.

Ruby Rae

October 6

Dear Diary,

I'm forging ahead. I told my best lady friend on the block. Today a bunch of teenagers spray-painted "faggot and freak" on the front of my house. I just wanna lie down and die. What I really want is Carolyn ... but I know this would be the final straw with her...

Ruby Rae

October 10

Dear Ruby Rae:

Are you alive? Hello? Is anyone out there? We've had our fights. We've had our ups and downs. But they've never lasted like this. I have scoop. Lots of scoop! (It's about Molly. You'll enjoy hearing about it. I caught the little monkey in her own game, and I made sure that Meg knows I did. Getting sterilized was the smartest decision I ever made.) And I've been doing some writing, and some things seem to be happening careerwise for me. That short story you sold for me has opened many doors. Thank you from the bottom of my heart.

Carolyn

October 12

Mzzzz. Ruby Rae Stone,

THIS is the final straw! You send back my letter with a huge message written in your hand on the face of the unopened envelope. The scrawl says, "Return to sender, addressee unknown, no such number, no such zip code." Then, when I spring for an international phone call (which might seem like just like pesos for you but is big dinero for me, since I gave away my only house and only piece of good jewelry and I am reduced to living on savings and income from a few FREE-LANCE ASSIGNMENTS), you slam down the phone at the sound of my voice. Is that any way to treat your best friend and sister, whose life you helped turn into ruins? Of course not. So, quit acting as childish as a man, and write soon. I'm in desperate need of a few words from a real friend.

Carolyn

October 13

Dear Diary,

I've been out looking for agents. The news about me has gone around town fast. Nobody will even see me. My career is gone! What am I gonna do now?

Ruby

October 15

Dear Carolyn,

Since you obviously can't read between lines (even if there are no lines), perhaps you can understand this: It's over. There is nothing more for us to say to each other. I'm sorry.

Goodbye,
Ruby Rae

October 17

Ruby Rae,

Welcome to the Prima Donna's Club, dear. I knew this would be an easier mark for you to hit than the social register. Sorry, I just couldn't resist the jab. It's so wonderful to hear from you. I mean, now that we're writing, we're just steps away from fighting — which means that soon we'll have the air cleared!!! I knew you'd come through if I told you was in desperate need of receiving a few words from a real friend.

Anyhow, whether the air is clear or not, it's time to call a truce, because, girl, I've got scoop! Big, big scoop! I just received a special-delivery letter from Rick! He fell off the vine and hurt his back. While in traction, he realized he misses medicine. He'll return to what's left of his practice when fully recovered.

Also, he asked me back! He wrote, "Bruce was a means of fulfilling a sexual fantasy, whose reality was something other than expected." Although they were only together a short time, Bruce and he grew very fond of each other. But Rick assures me that Bruce sadly accepts the termination of their relationship. (Fortunately, Bruce had the good sense not to tell Shawn about Miss-Queen-for-a-Day-over-at-the-Knit-and-Sew. He's sold Queen Anne's Lighting & Lace, Ltd., and is off to live with Shawn in Italy. Poor Rick's having a hell of time trying to sell Miss Rikki's Knit and Sew.)

If I'm honest, Rick thinks I'll understand (if not accept) that at some point in our lives we all have bisexual feelings. He erred in following the instinct behind these feelings, because he deeply wounded me and Bruce, who feels Rick used him. Apparently, Bruce said it would have been more honest and kind of Rick to explore his sexual issues with a therapist. Rick now sees someone, and wants to work toward understanding all that happened between him and Bruce. He also hopes to overcome his fear of intimacy, so he and I can have a real marriage. (As if a man can overcome the fear of intimacy. With all the husbands and lovers I've had, I'm convinced this fear is one of those sex-linked traits. The scientists just haven't yet pinpointed it.)

After I digested this news (and the fact that Rick is either oblivious to, or chooses to ignore, my relationship with Conrad. Men can be such fools! Why do I have to be attracted to them? My life would be so much easier if I were a lesbian!), I wrote him a note on a king-sized box of Xerxes, his favorite condoms. It said: "The lover you once had in me long ago died. You'd best look elsewhere for the pieces you need to patch up your life." I asked him to find our dog, Petunia, and send her to me, along with a quit-claim deed to our house. Then I forwarded the condoms via Federal Express.

I hope all is well with you! I miss hearing from you. I miss the laughter that's tucked in your words. You're the only person I know who's insane enough to understand me. Don't leave me alone out here. My soul feels the mist of a fast-approaching madness that comes from bumping against nothingness.

Love,
Carolyn

P.S. Oh! And now, here is your scoop bonus: Rick dyed away his blond streaks, dumped the designer contacts, sent me his earrings, but — he's keeping the "i" and the twin "k's." That's right: it's still Miss Rikki.

October 20

Dear Diary,

I'm tired, real tired, and I just wish Carolyn would leave me alone. She's making it harder on me. I've been rejected everywhere, and I just don't have the strength to be rejected by her. You can only take so much in one life ... and I'm afraid one more little bit of heartbreak will drive me over the edge. The idea of suicide no longer flits across my mind ... now it saunters like my mother's girlfriend Ina used to saunter in a red fishtail dress and six-inch come-fuck-me shoes as she walked across a low-down tavern with a beer bottle in one hand and a cigarette in the other.

Ruby Rae

)ctober 25

Dear Ruby Rae,

I don't understand. What's happening with you? Are you ill? I'd rather know the truth. Not knowing is so painful. Especially now.

We've always fought. So you can't have broken off with me because I blamed you for causing the ruin of my life. We say the wrong things to each other all the time. In my heart, I fear that whatever it is, is serious. Very serious. Not knowing scares me. Do you really have a tumor? If you won't communicate with me, how can anything be resolved? You do want things to be resolved, don't you?

This morning I reread the last few letters you wrote to me. You said you'd reached a difficult place in your therapy. I was so busy thinking about myself that what you wrote didn't have an impact. Shit. I'm sorry about not focusing on what you told me. I guess in our last few letters we wrote at, rather than to, each other. Since I didn't focus on what you wrote to me back then, I'm all the more worried. If I hadn't been so selfish, I would have done a better job at reaching out to you. If I could do it all over again, I wouldn't overlook your needs.

Has Winnifred placed you in the hospital? Have you bitten into your skin? Have you used the wound's blood to scrawl bits of your madness across a locked room's white walls? If that's where you are, please understand that I, too, have explored the vast blackness that falls when truth and madness intertwine. And if you're lost in that abyss, I'll understand if you're unable to come back for a time. But don't fret. I'll be here, waiting for you as I wish you God's speed and pray that your journey brings you home safe.

These days, it feels as if I sleep against the spine of death while I wait for a lover to enter my life. This is the first time I've lived alone since I married at eighteen. I've never left a man without the safety of having another well-feathered nest to set myself up in. I hate the darkness in the night. It's forced me to realize I've peppered my life with Ricks and Hunters, who almost, but don't quite, meet my needs.

It's time for me to slow down and sort through things. So, if you don't hear from me, don't think I've surrendered to your whim to kiss off our friendship. If I don't get back to a safe place before you, reach into your soul while you wait for me, and feel the place where feelings live and die. If you reach in deep enough, you'll find that our friendship is still alive. Just hold on tight to that feeling till I get back to you.

I'd write I love you, but right now I'm unsure if either of us has a clear understanding of what love means.

Carolyn

November 10

Dear Diary,

Some teenager's scratched "faggot" on Kip's car. He's angry with me for telling the neighbor lady the truth about myself. He said, "Why did you have to tell everybody in the neighborhood the truth?" I hurt all over. To gain myself ... do I have to lose everything? How fair is that, God? I thought the nuns said You were fair? Well, I'll know soon. I'm coming to see ya. I can't take any more. I think I'll do it tonight. Tonight after Kip has gone to bed. I'll drive my car off of the Vincent Thomas Bridge into the L.A. Harbor.

Ruby Rae

November 10

Dear Ruby Rae,

I know, it's been a while since I've written. I haven't stopped loving you. But I've been busy meeting with my madness as it scratches against the still eyes of the night. The night's funny in the way that it uncovers what I hide from myself during the day. Who would think darkness could shed such light?

Intellectually, I've known for some time that I have the habit of entering into new relationships, and soon taking on the responsibilities that really belong to my lover. I feared if I didn't do this, he wouldn't like me, or want me. Once he became dependent on me, I resented him for being fragile, for needing my care, and never taking care of me or my needs.

This morning, just after midnight, I felt in the core of my being all of the anxiety that came from having wrapped my entire life around the concerns of not being good enough, or worthy enough, or special enough to deserve a relationship in which my partner and I freely give and receive nurturing care. The energy from this anxiety propelled me into a spin that shot me from my bed.

I tore from my house. I vaguely remember the cool touch of beach sand against the bare soles of my running feet. Clothed in a nightgown, I dove under the ocean's first set of moonless waves. I swam until I was so far out, and so turned around, that I couldn't discern the horizon from the shore. Disoriented, and frightened that I would die if I swam in the wrong direction, I floated on my back and searched the sky for familiar stars. And while I floated and searched, I was struck by the absurdity of having so often contemplated suicide when a husband or lover was unaware of my needs, and then, when faced with death, I wanted more than anything to live, even though there's no man in my life. As frightened as I was, I got a chuckle or two out of this.

On the wavering spine of this laugh there rode into my life the realization that in the face of Death, all humans are equal. And, because Death does not discriminate in whom it takes, how can I be any less worthy or deserving of love than any of the men who have littered my life?

The exhausting weight of caring for others and placing their needs before mine so they would stay with me had to go. If it didn't, its drag on my energy would prevent me from returning to shore. Certainly, if I wasn't good enough for some man to want and love, how could I be deserving of the energy needed to save myself? So, there, in the ocean's black vastness, I dumped my burden of "undeserving." Then I charted out the direction of the shore, and started swimming slow: swimming home. And when I reached the beach, I just sat, and breathed, and thought. I thought a lot. I sat until the sun came up.

On the beach, I realized the secrecy with which I handled my abortion and sterilization is a classic example of the way I never give men the opportunity to support me. I assumed Rick wouldn't be there, not because of who he is, but because of who I am. For too long, I've lived my life like a cork bobbing on the moonless waves. I've been much too self-contained, and too in control of taking care of me and all my needs. No wonder I always felt isolated from the men in my life. Feeling as cast off and adrift as I did, it's surprising there weren't more times when I contemplated suicide. Of course, in my suicidal rages, I always blamed "the man" rather than me for casting me out to drift in the sea. Must rage always tint the world in the wrong perspective?

Since returning to shore, I've come to understand and accept that I'm my mother's daughter. Like Portia, I too have a dependency. I'm a relationship junkie. And it's time I kick my habit. All of my marriages had the potential to be the relationship I've chased. But I never behaved in a manner that encouraged warmth, shared intimacy, or trust to flourish. I found it safer and easier to shore up emotional barriers than to blame my husbands for not doing the one thing I long ago should have done for me: namely, to demolish my self-serving shield of aloneness. On the outside, I appear to be a strong risk-taker, but on the inside, I crave safety and acceptance. I guess this doesn't make me much different from Portia. Like the saying goes, "the acorn never falls far from the tree."

How many times have I left a relationship saying, "He's not the 'right' man, who will make it 'okay' for me to crawl from my fear of intimacy?" It's always the man, never me, who traps me. He's always perceived as deficient in some small yet important way that makes him seem untrustworthy. Until I'm able to trust, to accept that it's my right to be vulnerable with people who care about me, I won't live a full life.

It's been a long, hard struggle to get to a place where I feel I deserve some decent, honest, and intimate loving; to accept that if I let myself feel vulnerable and open it doesn't mean I'll be abused. Just because I'm the product of an unlucky sperm flow, just because, as a child, I couldn't control my mother's physical and emotional and sexual attacks, my father's disinterest in the abuse or whether or not my uncle would choose to rape me on any given day, it doesn't mean that as an adult I can't now control who I let in my life, or stop inappropriate behavior directed at me.

Although I've forgiven Hunter and Portia and my uncle for their cruelty, I've yet to undertake the corresponding act of forgiveness. I need to forgive myself for not protecting myself from their abuse. I was physically and emotionally unable to rescue myself at such a young age. I can't be punished for not having skills no one could possibly expect of a child. And it's now a bad case of overkill to keep my defensive skills on red alert twenty-four hours a day as they needlessly keep at bay those who I need and want to come in and love me. What happened to me happened back then. But that was then, and this is the now. We live in the now, so why should I give them power over how I live my current life?

As for the way I hated men, and used and discarded them as I did, these were just symptoms of my problem. Men were never my problem. I was my problem. You were so right when you tagged me a control junkie. I couldn't just enjoy a man's company, I had to coldly and calculatingly turn him into a sexual object (such an enlightened thing for a "feminist" to do). Then, once he was my object, I tried to control him.

It deeply saddens (and embarrasses) me that while I could see that Bruce was kind, and loving, and playful (albeit, a tad more kind, and loving, and playful with Rick than with me), I turned him into an amusement park ride that was meant only to thrill me while I lay in bed. This diminished his relationship with Shawn, and showed a lack of respect for the courage and honesty it takes to live an openly gay life. Looking back, I feel terrible that I had such selfish thoughts when Shawn flew off to Italy. Bruce was in tears, but what did I see? Another man to manipulate for my own gain.

Granted, Bruce and I potentially could have spent the night baking oatmeal cookies, and talking while becoming friends. But we never could get close to this potential, because my control limited Bruce to never being anything more to me than a sexual fantasy. As for Morgan, I placed an advertisement for him as if I were looking to buy a preowned car or a couch.

My uncle turned me into his lust-object, and I didn't like it. So why should Bruce and Morgan (or Shawn, with his luscious salt-and-pepper chest hairs) like it any more than I did? And, for that matter, why should they have to pay the price for the way in which I was once treated?

As for Theresa and Conrad, well, when it came down to Conrad and me living together, I was talking in terms of closing a deal. You can't get much more icy than that. Well, yes, maybe you can. Theresa was a pawn who I generously "returned" to Conrad when I thought Rick was coming down here to prove his love to me. Oh, Ruby Rae, I'm so ashamed.

I've treated people so shabbily. But now that I've had a good cry, I can honestly vow to work toward not using people like this ever, ever, again.

In the ocean, I came face-to-face with nothingness, and when I did, I discovered nothing is something I don't need to fear. I have something more than nothing within me. Something, when pitted against nothing, makes nothing okay, even if the something within you is a small, frightened child.

As for what's happening (or not happening) between us, I'm just going to continue to write to you. I know my letters probably fly through your mail slot and land in the trash unread, but I don't care. I feel that if I keep reaching out my hand in the only way I can, your hand will eventually reach out and grab back. It has to. You're my very best friend, and soul sister.

Missing you oodles and oodles. I love you!

Carolyn

November 10

Dear Diary,

Not only am I an outcast, but I'm a coward. I can't drive off of a bridge ... not sober ... and thank God I don't drink anymore. This too shall pass, or so my sponsor in AA says...

I need Carolyn more than ever. I'm going to tell her the truth and if she can't handle it ... fuck her!

Ruby Rae

November 10

Dear Carolyn,

Your heartfelt letter has been much appreciated and read over and over again. There's a reason I haven't written back. I'm going back to Tucker on the nine o'clock plane. I'm taking these two letters to put on my daddy's and my mamma's graves. I have to share them with you, but before I do, there's something you must know. I am not a woman. I am a man ... whatever that is. I mean, biologically, and legally, I'm this thing they call a "man." But in my heart and in my soul I feel, look, and act like this thing they call a "woman" ... whatever that is. Now do you see why I haven't written back to you? While you begged for our friendship with your right hand ... with your left hand you squeezed me by the balls, saying you hate me for being born with these. You and the Fifth Fleet. The story of my life.

You see, when I was really little, Mamma was really crazy, and she used to either think I was her as a little girl or she would think I was my father. When she thought I was her, she used to sit me down and we'd play make-believe and I'd be her and she'd be her grandmother ... and she would drill me for hours on being the perfect lady ... sit like this ... talk like this ... smile like this ... never do this ... always do that ... and she'd promise me if I learned to be the perfect lady, my mother would someday come and take me home with her. See, when her mother gave her to her grandmother, that's what they told her: if she'd learn to be the perfect lady, her mother would come and take her home to live with her. Mamma tried real hard, but her mother never came. That's what happened to her. But that's not why I wear dresses and live my life as a woman.

Sometimes, Mamma would get me confused with Daddy, and she'd pull me on top of her and have her way with me. And when she wasn't satisfied, she'd beat me with whatever was handy. Those scars all over my body are from all the times she stabbed me or beat me bloody with whatever was handy for not satisfying her sexually. And as a four- and five-year-old boy I found it impossible to satisfy a 35-year-old woman, who was used to big dicks and hours of them. And I just learned early on in order to survive that when she sank into those depths of insanity and looked at me with the pain-iced eyes, she had to see herself, not Daddy. And make-believe comes easy to a child. So I just said, "Okay, I'm you," and that was that. And when I started school, being a boy was just another game of make-believe. And all of my life I just believed I was a woman ... even when I was on the wrestling team. Deep down inside I believed I was a woman. That's why I was able to get I.D. as a female ... 'cause I believed it. That's why I was so convincing. Do you realize that until a short time ago, all my life I sat down to pee? And poor old Bosco. He didn't die on top of me. One night while I slept he decided to undress me, and get on with the honeymoon, and when he did, he had a heart attack. I feel terrible about that.

Anyway, I know it's hard to understand; even for me it's hard. I know you must feel betrayed. But I didn't really mean to lie to you or deceive you. I really thought I was a woman up until a while ago, when I finally worked through to this point in my therapy. I expected Winnifred to be shocked, but she said that one day, early on in my therapy, I wore a short dress and no underwear and revealed myself to her while talking. She admits to being shocked that day.

Funny, I don't even remember that day. Anyway, she started to cry when I was able to verbalize my gender to her. She said they were tears of joy that had waited a long time to fall. Bless her heart.

Anyway, I know all this sounds strange. But until I started thinking about it, to me my penis was more a source of chagrin than identity; something to be tolerated and overcome as opposed to dealt with or acknowledged. Kinda like a beauty flaw, like a crooked nose, or a bad tooth. I love you, and I'll be back in about a week. I don't know why, but I've decided to take the train home.

Hope you'll be around,
Ruby Rae
(formerly, Reuben Ray)

November, forever

Dear Daddy,

Yesterday, I ran into my heartache and we stood there face-to-face. I could tell that pain was mine, by the smell of the oil and the gasoline. The oil and the gasoline from your torn-up and scorched old blue jeans. The blue jeans that you used to shed by my bed before you crawled on top of me. The blue jeans that you used to wear to the steel mill so that I'd have clothes to wear, so that I'd have food to eat. And I hate you and I love you.

You made me feel dirty, and you made me so ashamed that for years I didn't tell anybody, not even me. And I wonder if you really ever loved me at all. As painful as it is that you crawled on top of me, the most hurting part is that that's the only time you ever held me in your arms. That's the only time you ever kissed me.

And you never had any time for me. There was always factories, mistresses, crap games, whiskey bottles, and NBC's Game of the Week all in the line ahead of me. And it's no wonder I didn't want to grow up and be you. Nobody wants to grow up and be nothing ... and I assumed you were nothing, because every time I went to you there was nothing there ... except some toy to alleviate your guilt and throw the neighbors off the track.

And all my life you bitched at me for not "being a man," and the only time we ever spent alone you wanted me to be anything but that. Yeah, I know. You never really were certain that I was your biological child. But is that my fault, or your fault for marrying a slut? And there's two sides to a slut. I remember all those nights Mamma waited, crying at the window for you.

Whether I was your child or not, you had no right to confront me about it, to rape me in your drunken rages when you decided I didn't look enough like you or act enough like you. And most of all, if you were going to abandon me, then why couldn't you be man enough to just walk completely away?

And just one last bone. I lettered in two sports for three years in high school — wrestling and tennis — and I was president of the student body and an honor student and none of that was enough for you. No, I had to play baseball, because you liked baseball. And when I went out for Little League to try to please you, what did you do? Did you help me? Did you throw me one fuckin' ball? Did you hit me one goddamned fly ball? No. No, you refused to come and watch me play because I wasn't any good, and you were ashamed of me. And then I got cut from the team. I admit it takes some pretty awful playing to get cut from a Little League team, but I had done the very best I could, and that's all I could do, and I did it solely for you. I'm sorry it wasn't enough. I know you were disappointed, and your obvious disappointment was painful enough. You didn't have to get drunk and say I wasn't your son, and then smack me upside the head. And when I started to cry you called me a sissy, pushed me down on the floor and kicked me in the face and said, "Yo' mamma had three miscarriages, why couldn't she have had four?"

And, yes, I grew up to be a drag queen, but I did not order this life from Sears; still, I have to pay the bill. And how do you think I feel, when I see all my old school buddies with their wives and their families? And here I am out here on this dark, distant tangent, living in the shadows of life, holding on for dear life. Don't you think I miss the children that I'll never have; pine for my wife, whom I'll never know, because it will take all of my life and every drop of strength I can muster to stand guard over this bottomless abyss of despair, anguish, and rage that is me, after years of your abuse, because I may or may not have been your child?

But I forgive you. And I pity you. You, who were the real sissy; big dick, mistresses, firearms, macho ways, and all. I understand. You did the very best you could. I'm sorry that it wasn't enough. But I'll never smack you upside the head, kick you in the face, or wish that you'd been born dead because what you had to give me wasn't enough. I'll take my comfort in the fact that you did the best you could.

And even though I shouldn't be, I'm sorry. I'm sorry I wasn't enough. I'm sorry that you were ashamed of me. I'm sorry you were so uncertain as to whether or not you were my father. And this is the last thing that I can think of to do for you and for me. You don't have to be my father anymore. You are free now. You are no longer my father; I'll never bother you again. From this day forward, I will be my own father. Yes, it's late, and it's not much, but again, it's the very best I can do. I'll be loving you...

Always,
Ruby Rae

Dear Mamma,

You will get the blame, because mammas always do. But I understand. I was there; and the finger really should be pointed at anybody but you. But for some reason, just like when I chose you on the road, it is you that I choose not to be able to completely forgive. Don't ask me why. Just like on the road, it's just a forced truth from the heart. And, when it comes from the heart, it goes to the heart.

Granted, Daddy was more like some far-off Arctic sun, impossible to touch and even harder to reach, but you were like an angry sea who slurps up her sailor son and then spits his bones on some abandoned beach. Perhaps this is why my mind is like a judge who wants to set you free for the crimes to which you were only an accessory. But my heart is a jailor who won't turn the key, and so I wear your clothes like you wore me, Mamma.

In many ways, Catfyshe, I'm just a totem to you. And, yes, you beat me, you cut me, you burned me, you left me alone for days on end, you called me names, and you threw me out in the snow naked in the middle of the night ... but didn't I hear you cry one morning? Didn't I hear you call out your mamma's name? Didn't I hear you beg her to love you? Didn't I hear you ask when she was coming to take you home? Didn't you say, "But, Granny, I've been good, and you said if I was good Mamma would come for me today"? Didn't I hear you screaming in the bathtub ... something about being dunked down in the well? And didn't I see you standing naked in the darkness, reeking of whiskey, and whispering Willie's name? Didn't you stand there waiting for him at the window, all night long, Catfyshe, until the break of day sent you to bed wet with fear? It'd take a hard heart to hate you, Catfyshe. It'd take an awful blind man not to see the method in your madness, the wisdom of your ways.

That's why I've always loved you, Catfyshe ... even when I was almost dying from the things you had to do. Yes, perhaps the things the church ladies had to say about you were true, and, yes, the truth is just the light, but sometimes the light ain't in the day, it's in the night. And I saw you in the darkness, Catfyshe ... and that is why I'd be right proud to be looking like you and loving you ... always.

Ruby Rae (Yes, I took your mamma's name.)

November 12

Dear Diary,

I'm on the train back from Tucker. Little town after little town freckles the cornfields and fruit orchards of the Midwest, and in a way they all look like Tucker, full of houses with tar paper siding, and clotheslines bending from the heavy load of flannel shirts and faded jeans. Of course, you never see the good side of town from the train.

It sets me to thinking ... and now that I think about it some more, I realize what I feel most guilty about is not the times my parents made me sleep with them, but the times that I snuck into my father's bed and did him, while he lay there drunk.

That's right. I did him. I did him until he couldn't be done no more. I did him because Catfyshe used to say "a stiff dick has no conscience and no home, but a soft dick will never roam." And she couldn't love Willie enough ... and I knew that one of those nights when he was out with his mistress he was not going to come back home ... so I did him to keep him at home.

Yes, regardless of who I chose on the road, I loved him more than I could ever say ... and I only told him the truth because he told me to tell him the truth. And I don't ever remember having control of the truth. I loved him so much that I was willing to become Catfyshe, so I could do a more thorough job of loving him. I was better at it than she was. I packed his lunches. I cooked most of his meals. I sat on his lap and I shaved him. I cooled his burns from the spitting steel with cocoa butter. I rubbed his big aching muscles with alcohol. I scratched his back. I listened to his stories about how hard things had been in his life, over and over again. She was in no condition to do this. That's why he was out in the street. Because a wife has to be a chef in the kitchen, a lady in the parlor, a whore in the bedroom, and mamma the rest of the time ... and I was that, not because that's who I was, but because that's who he needed me to be.

And even though none of us knew for sure who my father was, I couldn't have loved him any more ... and I couldn't have loved him any less. Yes, I did what I had to do to make that tar paper shack a home. And I ain't proud, and I ain't ashamed, and I ain't innocent ... not by a long shot. Being born in that house, I couldn't afford the luxuries of innocence, pride, and shame. Innocence wasn't an issue; survival was the issue. It wasn't about shame. It was about a long, cold, hard winter coming, and needing somebody to buy coal. I didn't know nothing about not having pride. But I knew about not having milk. And at that age it just seemed easier to live without pride than to eat cornflakes with water.

Daddy hated me for what I was and for who I might not be. And I used to cry, thinking it's so unfair 'cause I did it all for him ... lies ... I did it all for me. Hey, I'm a survivor and there ain't no shame in that.

Yeah, kinda like this old tired earth, Lord, it seems I been spinning since my birth. It's no wonder I feel a might light-headed and confused sometimes.

Ruby Rae

November 12

Dear Diary,

I slept for a while, and the train has rambled out of the wheat fields of Nebraska into the endlessness that is Wyoming. I've been thinking. I've been thinking about Catfyshe. I looked in my mirror to check my makeup and I realized that it wasn't me in there ... it was Catfyshe.

Catfyshe was a madwoman. But I loved her so. She was Mamma. And here's some more truth. She loved Willie ... she just wasn't in no condition to do it right ... not with all of those hungry black bitches out there ready to pounce on a good man with a sturdy dick and steady paycheck like so many alley cats on a fat field mouse. So I came to Catfyshe's aid.

Part II of my confession: part of my doing Daddy was because I loved him, and I didn't want him to go. Another part was because I loved Catfyshe and I didn't want to see her heart broken. So I did what I knew she would've done, if she hadn't been being consumed by the rage.

Oh, and the rage ... I never talked much about it ... but I've figured out where it came from. My great-aunt Tula Rose told me the whole story. You see, Catfyshe's great-grandfather, Papa Luke (who raised Catfyshe's grandfather, her father, and Catfyshe), used to dunk her father, her grandfather, and Catfyshe down in the well when they were little children. He would tie them on a rope and lower them down in the well and leave them there for hours on end sometimes. He had a fixation with wells. Tula Rose said Papa Luke was born right after slavery time. His father, Beau, the son of a plantation owner, and his mother, Litty Pearl, the daughter of one of the house slaves, grew up in the house together. White master and black slave, true, but children nonetheless.

Anyway, Beau went away to prep school, college, and then the war. When he came home, a young man, he fell in love with Litty Pearl, who had blossomed into a beautiful young woman. Beau's family forbade the marriage. But Beau and Litty Pearl were in love, and so Beau left his family and fortune to live down in the colored flats with Litty Pearl.

Exile wasn't enough. The night riders came, and they tied Beau and Litty Pearl to a tree stump and burned them at the stake and then dropped their charred bodies down in the well. They did this in front of Papa Luke, who was just three years old ... "and that child wasn't never right since ... and that's why he was the way he was about dem wells," Tula Rose said to me, and then went off into humming a hymn ... like she had been waiting there in that nursing home all these years just to tell me that story, and now she could die in peace.

In light of it all, I'm glad I could love Catfyshe like I did. Even if I did do what I did. 'Cause it was the fire of the night riders that burned Beau and Litty Pearl that also consumed Catfyshe, night after night, as she disintegrated into madness. And for all practical purposes it was the violence and insanity of the Mississippi night riders that took over Catfyshe's eyes and ways when she came at me with a knife or a gun. But because the logical love that a child has for her or his mother is a little bit stronger than the irrational hatred of racism, I was able to escape the fiery rage of the night riders that was passed on in my family from hand to hand, like a wine bottle down south, passed on from man to man. I was able to douse the fire with love, and scatter the cinders with forgiveness. And like that old well, now boarded over and buried beneath a hundred years of agrarian tranquility somewhere in the moody Mississippi delta, there is a hole in me, also boarded over, that runs much deeper than the eye can see ... but no child shall ever dangle there in the darkness at the end of a madman's rope, like Catfyshe did. Yes, it was love that brought on the wrath of the night riders; and it is love that has driven it away.

And now looking back, I can see that doing my daddy to keep my family together was a sad, desperate political act ... like the Jewish mothers throwing their babies against that electric fence to keep them from the Nazis. Crawling into my daddy's bed and burying my face in his loins at age five was like being thrown against an electric fence. It took all my courage, and some might claim it killed my inner child. But I know I saved myself from something far more painful ... in the long run. Yes, I truly understand what the Jewish women felt standing at that electric fence. When faced with a hard call in an even harder world, there is but only one choice, and that is trust your instincts to be closer to God than any- and everything around you. And that is the hardest call.

Now, as an adult, knowing what I had the strength to do as a child, I have been able to find the strength to be myself and to forgive myself, my mamma, the fire, the people who passed it on, and the people who set it. That's right, I have forgiven the night riders. Not because I'm a saint, but for the same reason I crawled into my daddy's bed — because I'm a survivor. I know I would never be able to forgive myself if I had been weak and taken refuge in the childhood luxury of innocence and let Catfyshe and that tar paper shack fall down around me.

It's strange, I know, but a child and a man are like an acorn and an oak, and everything that's in an oak is in an acorn, and it really depends on the needs of the world around it whether an acorn is the end of an oak or the beginning of a tree. And so it is, and always has been, with the child, the man, and the woman in me.

Always and forever,
Ruby

VIA FEDERAL EXPRESS

November 15

Dear Ruby,

—or do you prefer the more anatomically correct Reuben Ray? (Sorry. But, this is going to take a while — you still do want to be called "Ruby," don't you? I'm so confused. I mean Ruby Rae is politically correct, but then, with the way you always add "esses" to author and actor, I suppose you might rather not be politically correct. And it is "she," isn't it? Not "he." I do so want to do the socially correct thing, and Miss Manners, well, I don't think she's ever included this problem in her etiquette column.)

First, I'm glad you're back. And second, this is one hell of a way to tell me Baby Kip is gay. (Married, indeed! — Does he know you shoved him out of the closet, and locked its door behind him? — Talk about outing someone! — Perhaps you are a tad more political than I thought. As for Kip being gay, I can't believe that out of three siblings, I have to be the straight one. Is there no justice in this world? Why me, Lord?)

When I've fully digested all this, you'll get my full reaction. But, for now, I'll just say, had I any inkling that you were a man — never in my right mind — we even talked about sex! I can't believe I sent you my *Playgirls*! And Mr. April was your favorite, too!

I guess, when you think of the way I've treated the opposite sex, my first male friend would need to enter my life in a dress. And don't you dare stop speaking to me ever again!

Loving you. The all of you,
Carolyn

P.S. And might I suggest that you get out a dictionary and look up the word "deceive"?

The Fall (need I say more?)

Dear Carolyn,

I'm surprised. You're handling this rather well. I mean considering how much you hate penises, well, most of the time anyway. Don't ask me why. I don't know why I take refuge in this aspect of my personality. I do know this, though: it's natural. It's what's comfortable for me ... I've been a long time coming to the painful realization that no matter how much therapy I have or how hard I try, I'll never be Wally Cleaver, and in this dress is where I'm supposed to be. Don't ask me; ask God.

I don't want you to confuse being gay with being a transvestite. Sexual preference has nothing to do with transvestism. Most transvestites are heterosexual men. (I'm surprised you haven't married one ... yet. Or maybe you have ... you'd better count the panties in your dresser drawer, doll.)

I also don't want you to think that I'm a transvestite or that I'm gay because I was raped by my parents ... I used to think that ... just a couple of weeks ago ... but to quote you, "to even Freud, sometimes, a cigar is just a cigar" ... no pun intended. I'm gay because I am, like you're straight, not because you were raped by your uncles, but just because you are. I'm a transvestite because this expression of my persona best suits me. I'm an artist because I was raped. I'm a compulsive overeater and alcoholic because I was raped. I'm a compulsive spender and my self-esteem slowly crawls up from the bottommost rocks because of the nights I spent between my parents. The healthiest part of me is the part that is gay. That's the only part of me that can love.

Now about deceit. Yes. I will look up *deceit* in the dictionary, if you promise me you'll look up *isolation;* you'll look up *solitude;* you'll look up *outcast*. There's no excuse for doing wrong, and deceit is wrong. But, time and time again, I've had friends walk away because I'm a man in a dress. And even though I am a man in a dress, I'm also a person in a dress, with the same human needs and emotions. So, you tell me ... am I wrong for trying to hold on to the best friend I ever had; am I wrong for trying to run away 'cause the pain would have probably been too bad had you, like so many others, turned your back on me?

So, what's it gonna be? Are you going to come for Thanksgiving? Are we sisters, or aren't we? Regardless of what you do ... I'll be loving you.

Always,
Ruby Rae (Reuben, indeed!)

December 3

Dear Ruby Rae,

I can't remember when I've had such an interesting Thanksgiving. Your turkey — it so reminded me of Peking duck (not that your bird tasted all that bad when you considered how it just shriveled up in that roasting pan.)

—And speaking of poultry, I hope you don't mind, but you know that turkey jerky you sent home with me? Well, I put it in a nice jar, and made a big pink bow for it, and gave it to Theresa and Conrad as a wedding present. They plan to keep it on Conrad's boat in case it ever runs out of fuel a hundred miles from shore, and he needs some bait for fish. I didn't know they were so into survival. I guess that's something your cooking just brings out in people: the instinct for survival.

Anyway, sorry about that hot cocoa I spilled all over the centerfold of your latest *Playgirl*. (It's so nice you finally broke down and bought a subscription. Personally, I think it proves you're getting to a healthier place. When you step off the deep end, trust me, I know lust is always the first thing to go.) I blotted up what cocoa I could, and you'll have to agree, I pretty much saved most of the good parts. (Not that there were many — that a man like him thinks he has something to show!)

It's so nice to have a male friend with whom I can share intimate secrets. And while I'm on the subject of nice, it's nice that you've been there for me, and have reached out like you have to help me overcome my fear of intimacy, and teach me that, yes, a man can really "be there for me." But, in truth, had you not come into my life in a dress, I never would be on this road that's going to take me to a place of trusting men. Thank you for being my friend. And a big double thanks for being a drag queen! — I think God placed you on earth just to come to my aid.

I love you to pieces!
Carolyn

P.S. Oh, as long as I'm saying my thank-yous, thanks for that horrible case of indigestion. Had you not cooked that last meal, I never would have had to make that trip to the hospital where I met just the most darling man. He's an emergency room doc (they have tons of time off). He just dropped me a postcard. He's coming to Cabos San Lucas next week! I'll fill you in later. And don't worry. I'm going to let this one get close to me. Real close.

December 7

Dear Carolyn,

Another doctor? The last time the medical profession encountered a scourge like you was polio back in the 1950s.

Furthermore, my turkey was flawless and you know it. The only reason it fell apart was because it was so juicy and tender. The differences in our turkeys are like the differences in us. Yours may look good on the outside but after the first couple of bites ... I won't go on. History speaks for itself.

Gave that turkey platter I sent you home with to Theresa and Conrad as a wedding present? Honey, considering you gave Theresa the groom for her wedding, don't you think you've given her enough gifts?

And about this gender thing, let's get this straight right now. Every time we fight ... even though I can't imagine us fighting ... I don't want you bringing up my genitals and trying to use them as a weapon against me ... so let's get this straight right now ... I'm more man than you'll ever have and more woman than you'll ever be ... so don't try it. Thanks for the nice gifts, especially your presence.

Write soon,
Ruby Rae

P.S. Speaking of Peking duck ... is there anything they can do for those lines coming in your neck?

THE BEGINNING

TO OUR READERS

We did not sit down with the intention to write this book. And after it was written, we were even less inclined to publish it. It was only after much thought that we decided this work ought to be shared with the many others in this world who are forced into those remote places of refuge where most people never go. For you who have experienced the harsh extremities of this life, let this be a testament to the fact that if we can forgive, we can survive. There are no victims, only volunteers.

Like this tired, troubled Earth, our parents gave us all they had to give and all that we needed to carry on. Our husbands have provided us with everything our parents could not, including the stability we so need in our lives. We are blessed to have partners who love us in spite of our madness.

ABOUT THE AUTHORS

BILLI GORDON, a University of Michigan alumna, was born in Dowagiac, Michigan, and is the top greeting card model in the world. The recipient of the 1990 Golden Poet Award, her poetry has been included in various anthologies of contemporary American poets. Billi resides on the West Coast with her husband and their five children: Cocoa Puff, Dumpling, Robbie, Chip, and Ernie ... a springer spaniel, a basset hound, and three cats. She is completing her first volume of poetry.

TAYLOR-ANNE WENTWORTH attended private schools, and received a master's degree in sociology. She resides on the East Coast with her husband. She is completing a novel.

Other books of interest from ALYSON PUBLICATIONS

THE GAY BOOK OF LISTS, by Leigh Rutledge, $8.00. A fascinating and informative collection of lists, ranging from history (6 gay popes) to politics (9 perfectly disgusting reactions to AIDS) to useless (9 Victorian "cures" for masturbation).

WHAT I LOVE ABOUT LESBIAN POLITICS IS ARGUING WITH PEOPLE I AGREE WITH, by Kris Kovick, $8.00. The truth is funnier than fiction, especially when seen through the warped mind of Kris Kovick. These cartoons and essays look at religion and therapy ("I try to keep them separate, but it's hard"), lesbians and gay men, politics, sexuality, parenting, and American culture.

EMBRACING THE DARK, edited by Eric Garber, $9.00. Eleven chilling horror stories depict worlds of gay werewolves and lesbian vampires, and sexual fantasies that take on lives of their own. Contributors include Jeffrey N. McMahan, Jewelle Gomez, Peter Robins, Jess Wells ... and nineteenth-century gay rights pioneer Karl Heinrich Ulrichs.

CRYSTAL CAGE, by Sandy Bayer, $9.00. Stephanie Nowland used her psychic powers to put an escaped murderer behind bars in Bayer's first book, *The Crystal Curtain*. Now, she feels she must use those same powers against another lesbian.

LEAVE A LIGHT ON FOR ME, by Jean Swallow, $10.00. Real life in real time for four San Francisco lesbians: cold coffee in the kitchen, hot sex on the side, with friendships strong enough to pull them all through.

SOCIETY AND THE HEALTHY HOMOSEXUAL, by George Weinberg, $8.00. The man who coined the term *homophobia* examines its causes, and its disastrous but often subtle effect on gay people. He cautions lesbians and gay men against assuming that universal problems such as loneliness stem from their sexual orientation.

THE ADVOCATE ADVISER, by Pat Califia, $9.00. Whether she's discussing the etiquette of a holy union ceremony or the ethics of zoophilia, Califia's advice is always useful, often unorthodox, and sometimes quite funny.

THE ALYSON ALMANAC, $9.00. Gay and lesbian history and biographies, scores of useful addresses and phone numbers, and much more are all gathered in this useful yet entertaining reference.

BETTER ANGEL, by Richard Meeker, $7.00. Fifty years ago, *Better Angel* provided one of the few positive images available of gay life. Today, it remains a touching story of a young man's discovery of his sexuality in the years between the World Wars.

BI ANY OTHER NAME, edited by Loraine Hutchins and Lani Kaahumanu, $12.00. In this ground-breaking anthology, hear the voices of over seventy women and men from all walks of life describe their lives as bisexuals in prose, poetry, art, and essays.

BROTHER TO BROTHER, edited by Essex Hemphill, $9.00. Black activist and poet Essex Hemphill has carried on in the footsteps of the late Joseph Beam (editor of *In the Life*) with this new anthology of fiction, essays, and poetry by black gay men.

COMING OUT RIGHT, by Wes Muchmore and William Hanson, $8.00. Coming out can be frightening and confusing, but with this recently updated book it's a little easier for you, your family member, or a friend who's taking that first step.

THE GAY FIRESIDE COMPANION, by Leigh Rutledge, $9.00. A rich compendium of unusual and interesting information by the master of gay trivia. Short articles cover a wide range of topics. A favorite gift item.

IN THE LIFE, edited by Joseph Beam, $9.00. In black slang, the expression "in the life" often means "gay." In this anthology, black gay men from many backgrounds describe their lives and their hopes through essays, short fiction, poetry, and artwork.

LAVENDER LISTS, by Lynne Y. Fletcher and Adrien Saks, $9.00. *Lavender Lists* starts where *The Gay Book of Lists* and *Lesbian Lists* left off! Dozens of clever and original lists give you interesting and entertaining snippets of gay and lesbian lore.